Polly smiled br
interest in you
Will Survive, w
to most of the l
stores. They ha
year's ascent on ~~Everest too. And we all~~
know how they embrace equality on all
levels, don't we? This really will launch
you as a man of the moment."

"Do we? Will it?"

Tanya surreptitiously pinched Dom in his side.

Polly rushed on regardless. "They have a major presence in the LGBT community and are linked to many gay climbing clubs and events. They'll be thrilled to have representation from another openly gay celebrity." She was already directing Ellie to look up a contact number.

"Another?"

"They used the famous gay model Zeb Z for that swimwear campaign last year."

"Famous for what? Being gay?" Dom was still irritated, especially as things didn't seem to be going the way he expected. "There's no way you're promoting me for my sexuality rather than my work."

"No, no!" Polly's smile never wavered. "That's not what I meant. Just that I know now where to start pitching the campaign. You and Zeb Z. This is a *great* idea!"

Welcome to
 **REAMSPUN DESIRES**

Dear Reader,

Love is the dream. It dazzles us, makes us stronger, and brings us to our knees. Dreamspun Desires tell stories of love featuring your favorite heartwarming heroes, captivating plots, and exotic locations. Stories that make your breath catch and your imagination soar.

In the pages of these wonderful love stories, readers can escape to a world where love conquers all, the tenderness of a first kiss sweeps you away, and your heart pounds at the sight of the one you love.

When you put it all together, you find romance in its truest form.

Love always finds a way.

Elizabeth North

Executive Director
Dreamspinner Press

Clare London

ROMANCING THE WRONG TWIN

PUBLISHED BY
DREAMSPINNER
PRESS

Published by
DREAMSPINNER PRESS

5032 CAPITAL CIRCLE SW, SUITE 2, PMB# 279, TALLAHASSEE, FL
32305-7886 USA
WWW.DREAMSPINNERPRESS.COM

This is a work of fiction. Names, characters, places, and incidents either
are the product of author imagination or are used fictitiously, and any
resemblance to actual persons, living or dead, business establishments,
events, or locales is entirely coincidental.

Romancing the Wrong Twin
© 2016 Clare London.

Cover Art
© 2016 Bree Archer.
http://www.breearcher.com
Cover content is for illustrative purposes only and any person depicted
on the cover is a model.

All rights reserved. This book is licensed to the original purchaser only.
Duplication or distribution via any means is illegal and a violation of
international copyright law, subject to criminal prosecution and upon
conviction, fines, and/or imprisonment. Any eBook format cannot be le-
gally loaned or given to others. No part of this book may be reproduced
or transmitted in any form or by any means, electronic or mechanical,
including photocopying, recording, or by any information storage and
retrieval system, without the written permission of the Publisher, except
where permitted by law. To request permission and all other inquiries,
contact Dreamspinner Press, 5032 Capital Circle SW, Suite 2, PMB#
279, Tallahassee, FL 32305-7886, USA, or www.dreamspinnerpress.
com.

ISBN: 978-1-63477-371-3
Digital ISBN: 978-1-63477-372-0
Library of Congress Control Number: 2016912692
Published November 2016
v. 1.0

Printed in the United States of America
∞
This paper meets the requirements of
ANSI/NISO Z39.48-1992 (Permanence of Paper).

CLARE LONDON took her pen name from the city where she lives, loves, and writes. A lone, brave female in a frenetic, testosterone-fueled family home, she juggles her writing with her other day job as an accountant.

She's written in many genres and across many settings, with award-winning novels and short stories published both online and in print. She says she likes variety in her writing while friends say she's just fickle, but as long as both theories spawn good fiction, she's happy. Most of her work features male/male romance and drama with a healthy serving of physical passion, as she enjoys both reading and writing about strong, sympathetic, and sexy characters.

Clare currently has several novels sulking at that tricky chapter-three stage and plenty of other projects in mind… she just has to find out where she left them in that frenetic, testosterone-fueled family home.

Clare loves to hear from readers, and you can contact her here:

Website: www.clarelondon.com
E-mail: clarelondon11@yahoo.co.uk
Blog: www.clarelondon.com/blog
Facebook: www.facebook.com/clarelondon
Twitter: @clare_london
Goodreads: www.goodreads.com/clarelondon
Amazon: www.amazon.com/author/clarelondon

To my readers, in the hope they have as much fun reading the story as I did writing it!

Chapter One

DOMINIC Hartington-George poured four sachets of sugar into the indistinguishable hot liquid they served in these premier London-address offices and sighed to himself. Sitting on his own in the luxuriously carpeted foyer, he wondered if he could work the Tardis-clone vending machine enough to get a chocolate bar as well.

On the pretext of needing a piss, he'd escaped from the meeting currently going on between his agent, Tanya Richards, and his PR company representatives. Well, he hadn't said that exactly, as Tanya had already briefed him about his language needing to be more socially acceptable. Apparently he wasn't on the top of a snowcapped mountain at the moment, where no one cared how he expressed his bodily needs except for the odd passing llama.

Dominic wondered idly why a llama's company felt infinitely more attractive compared to the meeting. And as an experienced mountaineer, he'd met a few llamas in his time. But he couldn't do anything about today, could he? He couldn't run away like he usually did—or as Tanya and his mother accused him of doing—to some mountain range to hide himself in another wild adventure.

Because he was broke.

Not only that, but he was hawking his begging bowl around London in the hope of a sponsorship deal. He had to endure long meetings, cheesy smiles that set off a cramp in his jaw, and daily spreadsheet reminders of just how much money was involved in climbing the Eiger. It all just emphasized the size of the shit pile he was in. What was more, he struggled to cope with negotiation at the best of times. In fact, he was beginning to think he'd be better suited to standing outside on the street and offering copies of the *Big Issue*. He was no bloody good at bowing and scraping. Wasn't that what he employed Tanya for, anyway?

"It's a necessary evil," she'd told him firmly. He'd just announced his next expedition, and *she'd* announced a resounding, financial no-can-do. "You may have an aristocratic name and impeccable pedigree, but—"

"Bugger-all money?" he'd interrupted almost gleefully. For centuries his family had been famous for being adventurers—and infamous for gambling away every treasure they had ever owned. Great-Grandad had wasted the final thousands of the family fortune on a rangy horse in the Epsom Derby that, rather than romping home at 200-1, had fallen over its own feet in the first fifteen yards and had to be put out to grass. After that, the surviving Hartington-Georges moved to their more modest London properties and lived on the erratic income from opening their ancestral home to the public. Dom suspected his elegant sophisticate of a mother had never got over the shock of a stranger approaching her one afternoon and asking to be escorted to the baby-changing facilities.

Tanya had continued, "So if you want to continue your mountaineering projects—"

"No question!" he'd snapped.

Tanya had just inclined her head, unfazed. She hadn't worked for Dom for two years without learning "his ways." "So we must look at ways to raise the funds. And one of those is through sponsorship deals. Take that disgusted look off your face, Dom. A lot of sportsmen and explorers do that nowadays."

"Climb mountains with a big yellow M emblazoned on my forehead?"

Tanya let a smile tease the corners of her mouth. "I think it'd be more suitable if the sponsor was in the outdoor clothing and survival equipment market. I have contacts I can approach."

Tanya always had contacts. Dom had to admire that in her. Also her ability to manage her insolent runt of an assistant, Eric—oh, and her ability to cope with Dom in full grumpy mode. There weren't many people who managed to do that. His own mother only dropped into his Ladbroke Grove house a few times a year. Otherwise, they were both happy to keep contact to the occasional phone call or bumping into each other at family friends' events.

"You need to come out of your shell," Tanya had said to him. That was an hour before she employed the PR company. "And that doesn't include dancing on a pub table to karaoke."

Bloody hell. If having a night out with his climbing mates wasn't coming out of his shell, Dom didn't know what was. At the end of a training week in North Wales, he'd needed to unwind. A visit to a familiar and discreet London pub around the back of Kentish Town, where the licensing hours were applied loosely, if at all, had been just the thing. The food was plain, plentiful, and delicious, though the karaoke machine was a new addition. Dom had tolerated it only because it promised a set of old rock classics. He'd been halfway through a roaring-drunk rendition of "We Are the Champions" when he'd been snapped by one of those damned paparazzi, passing by on the off chance of a story. And yes, he had been standing on the table at the time, but the landlord didn't care, so why should anyone else?

But apparently that wasn't the right *kind* of shell-emerging. "Other options?"

Tanya had looked him in the eye and said wryly, "Get a job. You know, like the rest of us mortals."

Dom had felt physically sick. Not at the thought of hard graft; he was used to that and was no coward when it came to rolling up his sleeves. But the thought of sitting in an office in a suit and tie, shackled to a computer for eight hours a day, and answering to *someone else....*

He'd shuddered.

So here he was now, in the plush offices paid for by poor saps like himself and the companies who branded them, trying to rebrand Dominic Hartington-George.

It was time to face the music again.

DOM had hoped to sneak back into the conference room with his coffee (tea? rat's pee?), but everyone turned to face him as he took his seat again. Tanya frowned at him, and Eric had that habitual smirk on his face, as if Dom were the greatest entertainment since schoolboys painted glue on the teacher's chalk. Of course, Dom thought rather glumly, that might be true, even if chalk had given way to an iPad stylus.

Two virtually interchangeable, slick-looking blondes in brightly colored, tightly fitted skirt suits and matching pearl earrings represented the PR company. One of them blushed every time she looked at him.

She was the first to speak. "Tanya says you're looking for a makeover. You know, like they do on the TV? *10 Years Younger*, *Look Good Naked*, that kind of thing?"

What was this modern habit of talking in questions all the time? Dom stared at her steadily until she blushed again. "I have no idea what you're talking about," he said bluntly.

"I mean… obviously you don't need help with your looks," she stammered.

Ah. That explained some of the blushing. He often got that with younger women. If he turned his head, he would catch sight of Tanya's frown moving to a whole new level of disapproval. It was almost enough to cheer him up.

"Just the presentation," the other girl said, more sharply. The young one looked at her with naked gratitude. "We'll get someone on his wardrobe. Ellie, look into a suitable hairstylist too."

"Hairstylist?" Dom switched his glare to her. Polly, he thought her name was. He reassessed her as more assertive than just slick. Was that why his death glare didn't work as well on her as on other people?

Polly raised an eyebrow at him as if she could hear exactly what he was thinking right then, and she was far from intimidated. "And let's now address the, shall we say, *thorny* issue of social image."

"What the hell does that mean?"

Polly didn't even flinch. She was obviously used to stroppy clients.

Tanya touched his arm. "Dom. Please. You want your funding, don't you?"

"But why does it matter what I look like?" He could hear the plaintive note in his voice; he sounded like a petulant child. But he didn't want to be bothered with this. "I climb rocks and mountains, ladies. I wear bulky, padded clothes and thick-soled boots. My face is usually covered with goggles or a mask against the sun and dust. I grunt and curse and fart. I see no reason for social chitchat, I eat like a hungry horse, and I don't— repeat, don't—*moisturize*."

To his surprise Polly laughed. "I hear you, Mr. Hartington-George."

"Call me Dom," he said grudgingly.

"You're a fine man, Dom. Handsome and assertive and brave. We know all that."

They do?

"We're just looking for a way to brand you so that other brands want to match up with you. They'll pay for that privilege, you see. And that means making you look even more attractive."

"And more amenable," Tanya said half under her breath.

Dom couldn't say he hated Polly's style of flattery, but he was still wary. And he supposed he hadn't spent much time or money on his looks for a few years now.

"What about a girlfriend?" Ellie asked timidly.

Dom started.

"If the client were seen with a suitable partner… someone already media-friendly…."

"The intrepid adventurer captured and tamed by homespun beauty? Great idea. It'd certainly build a marketable strapline." Polly nodded and started scribbling on her notepad. "We have Alisha W already on the books. And I believe Suzie de Luca is in London for a shoot."

"No thanks." Dom's deep voice sounded very clear in the room.

Beside him, Tanya closed her eyes.

"Well, if not them, there are plenty of other ladies who'd love to be seen with you," Polly continued, unconcerned. "It'd be just another assignment, of course…"

"Of course," Tanya echoed, her voice rather faint and her eyes still closed tight.

"…although we would expect you, Dom, to look happy with the arrangement on photoshoots and at public events. Meanwhile, it'll be excellent publicity for both of you, and you may even build a little romance, while persuading the media that the Daredevil Man in the wild can also be the Doting Man at home."

"No thanks," Dom repeated slowly. "Maybe that would be fine if you hadn't missed the whole point. The point that, even if I had time for dating, I don't date women."

Tanya leaned forward over the conference table and sank her head into her hands.

Eric snorted. Dom hoped it was because of nerves and not ridicule, else he'd thrash the kid when they got out of here. Eric was in his early twenties, overkeen, too bold, and completely unfazed by Dom's gravitas. And he had the most disrespectful sense of humor Dom had ever known, even though it made him laugh.

Ellie's eyes had opened very wide. "You mean you're gay?"

"You're choosing *now* to come out?" Tanya muttered.

"It's not a matter of coming out!" Dom snapped back. What bloody century did these people live in? These city types were meant to be alert to the whole modern-world thing. "I've never been *in*. I just don't choose to expose my love life to every bloody person on the planet."

"If you had one to expose," Eric mumbled.

Dom glared at the kid, but Eric returned the stare without fear. *Bugger.* Dom should never have invited Eric on that mates' night out, or confessed in his cups just how bloody long it'd been since he, Dom, had dated anyone—man, woman, or llama. Meanwhile, the rest of the room was deathly silent.

Then Polly laughed again.

Laughed? "Something amusing you?" Dom asked icily. He pushed his chair back, ready to leave.

Tanya made a small sound of distress, but Dom was just thankful this would be the end of the whole stupid, misguided campaign—

"That's perfect!" Polly smiled broadly. "I've already had interest in your expedition from We Will Survive, who supply climbing gear to most of the London exhibitions and stores. They have a contract for next year's ascent on Everest too. And we all know how they embrace equality on all levels, don't we? This really will launch you as a man of the moment."

"Do we? Will it?"

Tanya surreptitiously pinched Dom in his side.

Polly rushed on regardless. "They have a major presence in the LGBT community and are linked to many gay climbing clubs and events. They'll be thrilled to have representation from another openly gay celebrity." She was already directing Ellie to look up a contact number.

"Another?"

"They used the famous gay model Zeb Z for that swimwear campaign last year."

"Famous for what? Being gay?" Dom was still irritated, especially as things didn't seem to be going the way he expected. "There's no way you're promoting me for my sexuality rather than my work."

"No, no!" Polly's smile never wavered. "That's not what I meant. Just that I know now where to start pitching the campaign. You and Zeb Z. This is a *great* idea!"

Chapter Two

A GREAT idea?" Dom was still trying to get his head around it. "That now you're trying to organize a blind date for me with someone I've never even heard of? Won't this Zed person—"

"Zeb. Zeb Z. He's always excellent press—"

"Won't he be just as pissed off as—let's take a wild guess here—as *I* might be?"

Polly's eyelids flickered, and her gaze darted between Tanya and Dom. "Why would he?"

"You're talking about setting him up with me, to go out on a date, to be seen romantically together—"

Polly and Ellie burst into loud laughter. Dom stared at them, wondering when he'd stepped into the Twilight Zone. There was no other explanation for being surrounded by lunatics like these.

"Zeb will know it's only a game," Polly explained. "Of course he will! He'll do anything for publicity."

"He... what? You mean he'll date a complete stranger for the sake of self-promotion?"

Polly didn't even credit that with an answer. She just continued beaming at Dom as if he'd made the greatest joke this side of "a man walks into a bar."

Dom glanced over at Tanya, and she gave a small shrug. She looked as bemused as he did, though decidedly more resigned. However, Eric—damn him!—was nodding along with Polly's words.

"He's a serial dater," Eric said to Dom, with the confident assurance that came naturally to most media people under twenty-five. "I read it all the time in the gossip magazines. He's a good-time—" He paused and smirked happily at Dom. "—a good-time *guy* it'd be in this case, wouldn't it?"

"I'll chase you down one night," Dom muttered back, "and throw you and your sick jokes off a cliff."

"Gotta catch me first, old-timer," Eric said airily and turned back to Tanya.

When Ellie also turned to Tanya and started gabbling away about Zeb Z's schedule, Dom tried to tune out all the nonsense.

No such luck. Polly's voice broke into his reverie. "Dom? May I remind you"—Dom bit back the "hell no" that sprang to his lips—"that you still need that makeover? Maybe we can arrange a personal shopper? A stylist?"

Eric snorted. *Again.* "Good luck with that."

"Whatever." Dom didn't even have the energy to bite their heads off. "Sort it out with Tanya. I'll wait outside." He wanted out of there, and fast. He knew he came across as a grumpy old beast, but to be honest, he felt more weary than angry.

All he'd ever wanted to do was travel, and ever since he was in his teens, his wanderlust had nagged at him. The reputation of his explorer ancestors was in his blood. To his mother's eternal disappointment, he'd barely scraped through college, but he earned enough exams to get him onto the staff of an Outward Bound center. He then spent every spare moment training and studying his true passion—climbing. Finally he'd been accepted on some overseas events. Then slowly he worked his way onto more ambitious teams, and eventually he ran his own expeditions.

That was what he loved, where he really felt comfortable and as if he belonged. Out on the mountains, unencumbered by what others called civilized life, at the mercy—and the glory—of the elements. Pushing across challenging terrain, finding his way without the benefit of GPS, calling his own schedule, and concentrating fully on the rewards of surviving with nature. He wanted to be there, not here in a plush office with diamond-cut glasses of artificially sparkling water and fruit sliced into exactly the same-shaped pieces.

He pushed his chair back again, and this time he got as far as the door before Polly called to him.

"Thanks for your honesty and cooperation, Dom. I really think this is going to be a wonderfully high-profile opportunity for us all."

"Oh Jesus," he muttered under his breath. To him, it had sounded more like a death knell.

"DOM?" Tanya inched her way along the corridor toward the foyer. She had the kind of look on her face that wouldn't have looked amiss on a lion tamer, approaching the wildest beast without a chair or whip in her hand.

Dom had perched himself on one of the ludicrously uncomfortable plastic benches, designed by someone who obviously had a much smaller frame—and a less padded arse—than Dom's. He sipped at another cup of generic liquid from the vending machine. It might be green tea this time. Like he cared.

Tanya sat beside him. "It'll be all right."

Dom bit back the sarcastic response to that. He had nothing but sympathy and respect for Tanya, putting up with him for the last couple of years. His mother had persuaded him he needed a personal assistant for the promotional aspects of his career, even while he protested he needed no such thing. But his mother, who would have preferred a chief of industry or, at the very least, a barrister for a son, had gone ahead and employed a PA for him.

Tanya had coped with booking his trips, liaising with embassies and officials throughout the world, and handling newspaper stories and interviews on both radio and TV. Dom loved sharing news and photographs of his trips, and he considered himself a pretty decent photographer, with several illustrated expedition accounts already published. But he abhorred the idea of being a media personality. And that came across pretty obviously with anyone he met. Tanya had become his first line of defense and the person who soothed all those he offended. Insult was his natural talent—he'd told her so on her first day. And ever since then, she'd made it her personal mission to prevent him getting away with it.

"Sorry for the impromptu announcement about my shockingly minority love life," he said with a scowl. "But it's better they know what they're taking on, right?"

"Right." She smiled. "You're a whole package, Dom."

Dom had known he was gay since he first became aware of his sexuality. It had never been anything to make a fuss about. It wasn't until he was well into his teens and heard the horror stories from some of his gay friends that he realized how twistedly certain sections of the human race viewed it. From then on, Dom had learned to keep that side of his life to himself.

Not that there was much to be discreet about. Eric's snide comment had been right: Dom's love life had been barren for a long time now. When did he have the time to date? Or the appetite? Apart from the occasional one-night stand, the men he met were either singularly uninterested in him, or uninteresting to him. The whole bloody thing was a lottery, and the odds were stacked against him now he'd passed thirty-five.

"Anyone around at the moment?" Tanya asked quietly. "If you're already involved with someone, I'll alert the agency at once. You have every right to your private life."

"No. No one right now."

There weren't any social obstacles; his parents had never had any problem with him dating men. There was a precedent in the family, though his mother rarely talked about Great-Uncle Godfrey, except to bemoan that he'd been the one to tempt Great-Grandad into gambling in the first place. But God only knew, even if he found a man he could bear for more than an hour socially, Dom didn't want all that sappy stuff: the hearts and flowers, the rings, the stable home life. Why the hell did they think he climbed mountains and dug his way through mud-sodden valleys? It was to escape all that boring domesticity. Dom craved excitement, but it had never been through his love life. He'd never found a man who gave him that zest.

"I'm just acting like a spoiled child," he admitted ruefully. "But I don't want to have to spend time with some…."

"Some?" Tanya nudged.

"Some tabloid twink," he muttered. "Some effete airhead without a scrap of interesting conversation, who's never been adventuring farther than Hampstead Heath, and who's more interested in their shoes than—"

"Than you?"

He had the grace to laugh at himself. "Dreadful arrogance, isn't it?"

"No." Tanya's voice was gentle. "You just know what you like and don't like. And you're not very good at hiding it."

"I don't see the point. It's not my scene, Tanya. Clubbing and flirting and… whatever modern men do." Surely the expectations of his twenties and early thirties were all behind him now: the hope of finding a suitable partner, but then the increasingly depressing progression of meet, touch, repel. He could cope with the occasional ache of loneliness. That was what a set of new maps was for.

"I know, sweetie. But sometimes we have to make compromises."

He caught an undertone in her voice that surprised him. "And I guess that's what you do with me all the time, right?"

She chuckled. "Yes, you grumpy old git, it is. Good thing I like you, isn't it? And I want you to be able to do what you love, which is travel, and explore, and discover new experiences."

"Bought a lottery ticket, did you?"

She thumped him on the arm. "You think I'd give you my winnings if I won? Let's give the agency their head on this."

"You really think it's necessary?"

"Yes, I do." She bit her lip. "Dom, you're a really great guy. You just hide it too well."

He shifted uncomfortably on the wrecked ship's hull. "You think this'll work?"

"For God's sake, who knows? You're a commitmentphobe, without a shred of visible romance in that snowcapped heart of yours. I know being seen on the town with a sexy young thing in skintight designer jeans is the last thing you'd choose to do with your Saturday night—" She sighed and nudged her head against his shoulder. "—but if it'll get you the attention, and therefore the funds you need, it's worth a try."

Dom decided to let the insults pass. After all, they were all true. "How long do you think I'll have to put up with it? *Him*?"

She laughed. "It's just for a few social events while you're in London. It's not as if they're asking you to go out with a rabid llama."

There was that llama again: the one Tanya was so fond of mentioning. He'd opened his mouth to protest his preference for the simpleminded animal when Tanya slapped a hand over his mouth.

"And you never know," she said firmly. "You may enjoy it!"

Chapter Three

AIDAN Vincent stared at the letter in astonished horror.

> *We regret to inform you that despite our earlier preliminary discussions, the London Lane Theatre will not be available to host your production of* For His Eyes Only. *We apologize for any inconvenience this may cause. We were initially very interested in the concept. However, we had already booked August for a crossover comedy-drama starring two popular actors from television.*
>
> *They recently featured in the reality show* I'm a D-list Celebrity on a Desert Island *with a ballroom-dancing quiz-show presenter who bakes in his spare time.*

Okay, so that final sentence wasn't a direct quote from the letter, but Aidan knew it would be the real reason behind the cancellation of his pitch. Apparently it was TV celebrities who sold theater seats, not the content of the show. The London Lane had been the last hope on his list of theaters that would consider his new play. They had a reputation for hosting new playwrights and bringing fringe theater to the capital. As his part of the deal, Aidan had a new play all ready to go, including a small company of players who'd joined him in a local amateur group and were already half-rehearsed in their parts. It had seemed a great match.

Please keep in touch, the theater finished their letter. *We always welcome approaches from new local talent.*

But not this year, apparently. His heart sank with the last hopeful bubble of his dreams.

"What do you think, Aidan, love?" Wendy Rackham's soft, breathy voice broke into his tortured thoughts. "This head cold makes my voice too low to get a real sense of Erica's part."

"Sorry?"

"Aidan?" She put a hand on his arm, her delicate perfume wafting lily of the valley under his nose. "Are you all right?"

The actors from the Dreamweavers theater group were all crammed into his small flat in Twickenham for another read-through of the play. There were only three of them, but all were a mainstay of Aidan's work and loyal to his direction. And after all, new plays were put on with smaller and smaller casts these days. *Ben-Hur* was unlikely to be shown in a London theater anymore; patrons were lucky if they got a full *Twelve Angry Men*. For each of Aidan's productions—and there'd been an impressive dozen of them since he left drama school six years ago—the company did the initial readings

and editing over casual evenings at Aidan's flat, then
followed up with rehearsals at the local pub, the
Plough, or a nearby school where one of Wendy's many
nephews taught. When the play was finally ready to be
performed, they hired the tiny function room upstairs at
the pub. It wasn't the ideal venue, with raucous laughter
echoing from the bar below and the frequent groaning
of the toilet block's plumbing, but Aidan and his troupe
had done their apprenticeship with pride, with plans to
break into off–West End one day.

But now what?

He felt nauseous. Now they'd be back to square
one, begging the use of the school hall and pub function
room, performing on carpets ingrained with beer or
against a backdrop of an atlas of the world and the
latest GCSE results.

"What's up, Shakespeare?" Titus Regis bellowed
from over on the sofa, where he was squashed up
against the youngest member of the troupe, Simon Scot.
Titus looked as if he was enjoying both the proximity to
young blood and Simon's nervous hero worship, even
if the latter had never been acknowledged publicly.

Titus was Aidan's leading man: tall, dark, and
striking, in his midforties, with a small horse-breeding
farm in Surrey. Aidan could totally imagine him roaring
out commands across the paddock, because Titus's
voice rarely needed amplification. Whatever its effect
on stage, it was really useful for getting served in a
crowded pub.

"Nothing's up," Aidan said. He shoved the letter
into his jeans pocket.

"Crap," Titus boomed.

Beside him, Simon winced and clutched his copy of the script all the more tightly, his adoring gaze fixed on Titus.

"Darling…." Wendy fluttered with concern at Aidan's side. She was a gorgeous, middle-aged woman who struggled with playing maternal parts instead of her previous career performing pretty ingenues, however much Aidan praised her on her natural beauty. If they were out and about together in town, he had to steer her away from salons offering Botox injections. Though he was a bloody sight more tactful than Titus, who was fond of saying, "At least it's not the ugly sister for you yet!"

"I mean it. Everything's fine," he reassured her.

But it wasn't. He felt completely shaken. He had relied totally on the London gig to be his first step toward the West End. It wasn't as if he had aspirations for the London Palladium. His plays were gentle, witty comedies based on domestic life rather than overblown, glamorous musicals, but he'd have been thrilled to get a pitch in a real commercial theater. And his work was just starting to get a name for quality and wit after some complimentary reviews in the London suburban press.

Hard on the heels of his disappointment was the secondary, financial shock. The pub performances were fun but rarely covered costs. He'd needed the London booking, which would have been offered on a share of the box office takings. They'd have had access to a city location, established advertising, and use of professional props and costumes—and hopefully much better audience receipts. During school semesters he taught acting skills to kids at a Saturday-morning club, but he always struggled to stretch that income over the holiday periods. He could see working as a waiter in his

imminent future, or maybe a temp job at sale time in the
local department store.

Oh God.

Aidan wasn't the world's best at dealing with the
retail public, but what else could he do? Without some
support, there wouldn't be enough money for basics, let
alone luxuries like props and promotion. He was living
virtually hand to mouth at the moment anyway, since
he'd had to pay for a new clutch on his ancient car and
get the persistent damp patch in the kitchen fixed. Panic
started to rise like a physical lump in his throat. His life
and ambitions seemed to have derailed over the last few
years. Where had it all gone wrong? No money for light
and heat. *Food—*

"Sit down!" came Wendy's best schoolmarm voice.
She could project as well as Titus if the need arose.
"Aidan, do you hear me?"

"What's the matter with him?"

That was Simon, ever curious.

"Must be a panic attack," Titus announced.
"Haven't seen him go that color since I dropped the
skull into a pint of bitter during his *Hamlet, Questioning*
at the Plough in 2013."

Aidan was half pulled, half guided onto the sofa
beside Titus, who promptly shoved Simon off with
barked instructions to go and fetch a glass of water.
Then he busied himself plumping the cushions behind
Aidan's back. Wendy waved her hands around Aidan's
neck as if to loosen his tie even though he was wearing
his usual T-shirt. She gave a huff of confused frustration,
and her perfume wafted all over him again.

"Move it, Florence Nightingale." Titus held the
glass of water under Aidan's nose and jiggled it.

"It's not a panic attack. I was just taken aback." Aidan bit back a sigh. "Please. I'm not one of your horses, Titus. I can manage a glass of water on my own." He sipped at it, aware of the three pairs of eyes peering at him. Worry from Wendy, fascination from Simon—was he studying Aidan for ways to play a fainting character, for God's sake?—and Titus with a "there you are, all better now" bluff assurance. Aidan's heart sank farther. He had to tell his friends the bad news.

Here goes.

"We don't have the London Lane Theatre gig. They just confirmed it's already booked for August."

There was a moment of confused silence, and then a snort of disgust from Titus.

"But they promised that booking!" Wendy said.

"I know. But I suppose they have a better offer. I mean, a show that'll do better." He pulled the letter from his pocket and it did the rounds of the group, eliciting gasps and growls of disappointment and anger.

"You'll challenge this, of course," Titus said. "We had a verbal contract."

"Aidan." Wendy's look was surprisingly shrewd. "You can't just give up."

"Of course I won't," Aidan protested, but he could see she wasn't convinced. The trouble was, he was crap at selling himself under the best circumstances, and this was far from that. "I'll get us another venue."

"The pub?" Titus snorted. "We only had twenty people last performance, and two of them never looked up from necking the whole time."

"And what about costumes?" Simon was the unofficial wardrobe and general stage manager and also played supporting roles. "Ours are on their last legs. And the scenery we could have used? Lights? And—"

"I'll sort it all, okay? We'll have to do the rounds of charity shops again. We're no worse off than before." But no better either. The London Lane had been extremely supportive of him when they first discussed his plans, though Titus joked it was because the manager had developed a bloody huge crush on Aidan. So it looked like his personal charm had failed too. That shouldn't have been a surprise, judging by his previous, hapless love life.

"Do you want to continue the read-through?" Simon's question was as breezy as if nothing had happened.

"No." Even Aidan could hear his voice was wobbly.

Wendy smiled sympathetically at Aidan. "We've had enough drama for the night, I think. We'll see ourselves out. Call us when you want to schedule the next rehearsal." She stooped to kiss him on the cheek on her way out and murmured, "Don't be afraid to ask for help, darling. You can't always be the rock for everyone else to rely on."

Chapter Four

WHEN the buzzer announced another visitor to his flat, Aidan nearly ignored it. But maybe one of the troupe had forgotten their belongings. Titus's phone frequently fell out of his pocket and got stuck down between the sofa cushions. Aidan hauled himself from where he'd been lying morosely on the sofa, ran a hand through his hair to smooth it down, and dragged himself to unlock the door.

A young man burst into the flat with an unusually aggressive flourish. The door slammed behind him, and Aidan's huge collection of theatrical programs tumbled off the hall table with a thud as the visitor swept past toward the living room. The man spun around in the doorway; Aidan was close on his heels.

"Hi, sexy!" He wrapped two strong, lean, masculine arms around Aidan's waist and planted a sloppy kiss on his cheek. "I had a meeting at the Hammersmith studio, so I thought I'd drop in on my favorite twin."

"You mean your only twin? Hi, Zeb." Aidan struggled to take enough breath, but he didn't begrudge the hug and the kiss. That was just his brother's boisterous, effusive way. Aidan really appreciated the affection at this moment, but he admitted to himself this was one of the reasons he no longer shared a place with his twin. The dramatic turmoil was exhausting. "I'll put the kettle on."

"Excellent. All I've had to drink is vitamin water and a very indifferent bubbly." After another hug, Zeb darted away from him and peered at himself in the mirror over the fireplace. "Do you think the blond tips are really suitable for my coloring? And *Harper's* said they really need me with green contacts for the Iceland shoot."

From the kitchen, Aidan could hear Zeb but didn't bother answering. Zeb chattered on like this all the time, with no need for response. It was actually quite restful. And, as always, Aidan felt the lift of his heart that came with seeing his twin. It was as if they clicked perfectly back into place, however long they'd been apart.

"How did the meeting go? Was it an audition?" Aidan carefully walked back into the living room with two steaming mugs of tea.

"Sweetheart, you're the playwright. You're the one who holds auditions. Mine was just a chat with an agent and a marketing executive, you know?" Zeb waved a hand airily and plopped down onto the sofa; Aidan managed to move his mug of tea out of range just in time to prevent spillage. "An air kiss or two, a twirl of

the portfolio, and then it's Zeb, get your kit off to show
your abs."

"Zeb! Not really?"

Zeb laughed, a loud, uninhibited, totally entrancing
sound, though the effect was largely wasted on Aidan,
who'd seen Zeb practice it in front of the mirror more
than once. "Maybe I didn't have to strip off totally.
It's not always *that* kind of shoot. But there's no point
being coy about your assets in my business, is there?"

"I suppose not. I just don't like to think you have to
compromise yourself all the time." Aidan settled more
cautiously on the other armchair.

Zeb was one of London's most successful and
famous male models, but Aidan didn't feel totally
comfortable about his career, even though he knew
Zeb's success was as much due to his hard work as
his amazing flexibility of style. Zeb could play a
sophisticated businessman to advertise suits, then a
casual surfboarder in a wetsuit, with bleached locks. He
could model men's and women's wear, blessed as he
was with a fashionably androgynous look, and he could
expose or hide his "assets," as he called them, without
any shred of embarrassment. Happiness or misery
appeared at the snap of a photographer's fingers; he
could cry at will, smolder at a bowl of fruit as if it were
his naked soul mate, and look any age between sixteen
and sixty.

Zeb narrowed his kohl-rimmed eyes. "Compromise?
Now who's being coy? That's what business is, honey.
One big, sexy, cash-laden compromise from beginning
to end. What about you and your plays? As I remember,
you had to suck up to that London Lane crew to get
your latest place, didn't you? Including that theater
manager you said was leering at you."

"Who told you that?"

"You did, honey, when we worked through a couple of bottles of cheap prosecco to toast your success. And that opening date's in my diary, I promise."

"Don't bother." Aidan felt very weary. "Whatever compromises I've had to make didn't work."

"What?"

"There's no booking for my play. The London Lane turned me down. They don't want to work with me after all. An Aidan Vincent production won't be taking London by storm this year."

Zeb frowned. "But that's ridiculous. It was all set. You said they loved your work."

"It was. They did." Rehashing all the feelings of disappointment, Aidan began to wonder if Zeb's company was giving him more anguish than support. He really only got to see his twin every couple of months, depending on Zeb's traveling schedule, although they spoke often on Skype. "They'd seen a couple of the scenes we did two years ago in Vauxhall, when another of Wendy's nephews got us that open-mike evening at one of the clubs."

Aidan's work had been a great success there, maybe because of his inclusive range of characters, but it had been a free show, so they couldn't do that too often. And maybe it had made him overconfident.

"But you've worked so hard on it already."

Aidan was touched that Zeb had noticed. "Never mind." He forced out a cheerful tone. "I'll find another theater. Put on my own production." What possessed him to say that? That really *was* a pipe dream.

"Ade, honey, you don't have enough money for decent prosecco, let alone your own production. So when are you going to fight for these things?"

"Zeb, I don't need this." But it was true. What had Wendy said? She'd also accused him of giving up. "It just seems such a bloody struggle. Every year begging for audiences who really just want to have a quiet pint, scraping by on homemade costumes and charity-shop crockery. Reviews relegated to the corner of page ten in the local press."

Zeb frowned at him from the sofa. "What's up with you? You're really down. I thought you loved writing."

"So did I." Aidan had never really enjoyed acting, but writing plays? It had always given him a huge burst of excitement and pleasure. "I'm just tired. Ignore my whining." He knew he didn't need to put on a brave face in front of Zeb, but he couldn't seem to drop it. How sad was that?

With ridiculous grace, Zeb unfolded himself from his lounge-lizard position and dropped to his knees in front of Aidan. "Bro, your work's really good. It's just a matter of getting seen by the right people."

"I'd hoped this would be my chance."

"Then fuck 'em! I know plenty of people in the business. Let me put in a word for another venue. Get some celebrity support. Find sponsors for equipment. Pay for it myself, for that matter."

The wash of love and gratitude was almost more than Aidan could stand. "No! I mean, no thanks."

"Why the hell not? We're a pair, Ade, none closer. What's mine is yours, always."

Aidan had never admitted to his connection with the infamous Zeb Z, and amazingly no one ever tied them together in the media world. Aidan had his own theory of why that was. He reckoned Zeb was so bold and familiar from every major magazine that no one ever needed to know about his family, whereas Aidan was so low-key no one ever bothered to ask. They dressed and acted very differently, and had simply slipped into separate lives, at least as far as the public was concerned. Maybe they both had the dramatic gene in them, but whereas Zeb made the world his stage, Aidan was more than happy to be behind the scenes.

This had worked for them for many years, allowing them to follow their own dreams with little or no impact on each other's. Aidan had long ago learned to call his brother by his modeling name, Zeb Z. So much more exotic than Sean, wasn't it? And when Zeb managed to make it to any of Aidan's plays, he always came incognito. Yes, not only could he act any part a photographer needed, he could—just about, and only for a limited time, of course—play a nondescript face in a crowd.

And his support had always been unconditional. For Aidan, tears were ominously close. "I know you don't understand, Zeb, but I want to make it on my own. I want people to come to the play because it's me, not because I'm the brother of Zeb Z, the famous supermodel."

Zeb sighed. "What about grants? Bursaries?"

"There's nothing currently available for an amateur group with such a small reach. I write regularly to people and businesses for sponsorship or introductions, but no luck so far." Basically he'd used up all his stock of goodwill, and money was tight for everyone nowadays. Well, apart from Zeb.

"So tell me about the play." Zeb returned to his seat on the sofa, though not before patting Aidan's thigh in an avuncular way, an act he knew always made Aidan laugh.

"It's a comedy, actually, though not a laugh-out-loud kind of thing."

"I understand satire, bro," Zeb said wryly.

"Of course you do." Aidan smiled. "*For His Eyes Only* is a pastiche on the James Bond theme. The sexy guy saves the world and gets the other sexy guy."

"Hell of an elevator pitch, honey."

Aidan laughed again. "I just want to celebrate the changes in society toward LGBT people, you know? Not just the more somber side of diversity, although of course there's still the legacy of HIV, abuse, and sadness. I want to look at some of the more astonishing, good things that have happened, and in a gentle, tongue-in-cheek way."

"I know, bro. You've always managed to blend social issues with romcom, entertaining without boring the knickers off the audience. That's your big talent, and you deserve to be recognized for it."

Aidan was startled at the praise and knew he flushed. "Thanks, Zeb."

"How did the Dreamweavers take to it?"

"They've been really supportive. But most of them have bills to pay too. They need the company to find more success or they'll have less and less free time to give it."

Zeb sniffed. "I know you don't want me in your business, and astoundingly enough I haven't taken offense." He paused only to stick his tongue out at Aidan's similar gesture. He and Aidan often reverted to schoolkid behavior when they were together. "But there was a guy on my last shoot who was coaching us on acting like silent-movie stars. He organizes self-productions, you know? Both theater and—one day you'll be there, bro, one day!—the movies."

Aidan shook his head. "Thanks, but I can't afford all the upfront costs. There's hire of the venue, costumes, and staging to pay for. I need somewhere that'll work on a share of the takings, and even then it's a huge risk. I'll just have to forget it, for this year at least."

"Is your money situation that bad?" Zeb had an odd, pained look on his face.

Aidan was saved from having to confess, and—God forbid!—having to tap his twin for a short-term loan, by Zeb's phone ringing with a loud rendition of Madonna's "Vogue." Zeb grabbed it off the coffee table with surprising haste. "Sorry, I must take this."

Aidan nodded, glad for the distraction. He had to pull himself together, think up new plans.

"Zee!" Zeb answered with his calling-card response whenever anyone contacted him or asked his name.

Aidan winced at the volume, but fondly. Zeb was his twin, the other half of Aidan's own life. They lived separate lives, but they were by no means separate people. Theirs was a bond that would never break.

To Aidan's surprise, Zeb glanced his way, then leapt up off the sofa and wandered over to the window. He turned his back to Aidan and lowered his voice. That just wasn't Zeb's usual behavior, and Aidan was intrigued and a little worried. He stood as well, not sure whether to approach him. He couldn't hear the phone conversation, but he recognized the tightening of the muscles across Zeb's shoulders. Tension, worry. Why wouldn't Zeb share that with him?

When Zeb finished the call and turned back to Aidan, he looked studiedly neutral. "Honey, I have a favor to ask."

Chapter Five

OH *hell.*

Aidan knew what that look and phrase meant together.

It had been the same all through their lives. It meant he was expected to give Zeb his whole collection of fossils; it meant he had to take the blame for the three windows Zeb had broken playing slingshot; it meant he'd have to phone the school, pretending to be Zeb, to explain why he couldn't come in for science today when Zeb was actually sneaking into the latest movie with his older friends. Yet hadn't Aidan just been thinking about their indivisible bond, Zeb's support of his career? Zeb deserved his help in return.

"That depends," he said slowly.

"Thanks!"

"Now wait a minute." As Aidan anticipated, Zeb was taking it as a given. God, he loved his brother, and God, Zeb drove him insane! "Tell me what's going on."

Zeb's gaze slid away to his tea mug. "Oh, it's hardly anything serious. Have you… um… heard of Dominic Hartington-George?"

"The mountaineer? Of course I have."

Zeb looked startled. "*I* hadn't."

"Well, he doesn't exactly move in your circles, does he? And when was the last time you watched anything on TV apart from *Project Runway* or *X Factor*? There was a documentary only last month about the last polar expedition. Hartington-George wasn't one of the team, but they interviewed him about the training that would've been required. He's very articulate. Very experienced." Aidan wished the explorer had been given more screen time, but his input had only been for a matter of minutes.

"Jesus, Ade, you've got a really weird look on your face. Like you might enjoy doing a lunatic thing like that yourself."

"A polar expedition?" Aidan laughed. "I wish I had the courage."

"You climbed that mountain in Wales—"

"Snowdon, you mean. One of the mountains in the Five Peaks challenge. Lots of climbers do it." The look on Zeb's face said he believed it, but they'd all be certified lunatics as well. "So, what have you got to do with Hartington-George?"

"H-G? Hairy Guy?" Zeb's eyelashes fluttered exaggeratedly so that Aidan had to laugh.

"You can't call him that."

"Of course I can. Have you seen pictures of him? Great bear of a man. Usually got a beard, and *not* one of those cute goatee ones."

Personally Aidan thought the man was very handsome. Under his fierce-looking brows, he had lovely eyes that Aidan reckoned could look kind if H-G ever stopped scowling. He'd interviewed well on TV, his confidence quite obvious when talking about his favorite subject—mountains. But as soon as the interviewer had touched on H-G's own plans for the future, the scowl had returned and he'd shut her down almost rudely. They'd cut away from the interview shortly afterward.

"He's arrogant," Zeb said, obviously blissfully unaware of his own failings in that direction. "Obsessed with his bloody expeditions. Driven, with never a moment for anyone else. Or any*thing* else. It's no wonder he's run out of funds."

Aidan blinked. "I didn't know. I thought he was planning a trip to the Eiger or somewhere like that. I seem to remember an article in the *Guardian*…."

"Good grief, honey, you sound like a real fan! Do mountaineers have fans?" Zeb was chatting on blithely, ignoring the fact that his twin had flushed deep red. "Last I heard, he was found roaring drunk in a pub in Kentish Town, standing on a table with a pint of Guinness on his head, trying to sing every single verse of 'American Pie' to a karaoke machine."

Something about that vision made Aidan smile. "Sounds like fun."

"For God's sake, Aidan. It's the behavior of a pop star, not a mature outdoorsman. Even *I'd* have chosen Celine Dion. And apparently it lost him a sponsorship deal with a high-street clothing chain. I mean, would you buy high-spec climbing gear from such a man?"

Aidan thought privately he probably would, and he was amused that the outrageous Zeb Z, not known for modest behavior, found H-G so shocking. Was it because H-G was presumably older than Aidan and Zeb? Or considered part of the establishment because of his double-barreled pedigree? Aidan remembered reading that H-G could trace his ancestors back to Tudor royalty, but he couldn't shake the vision of Dominic Hartington-George singing at the top of his voice while balancing a pint on his head.

From Aidan's own experience of pubs in that part of London, he would bet H-G had been a huge hit. "He probably just wanted to relax. It's a dangerous life, and if he wants to let his hair down between trips—"

Zeb's expression grew mischievous. "What the papers don't know is that he was found shortly after that in the gents, in a clinch with one of the barmen."

"He's gay?"

Zeb shrugged. "Apparently so. Not my type, I must say, but others find him fascinating. I'm just amazed he's kept his private life out of the gossip papers up until now…"

"Because you'd know nothing about that," Aidan murmured.

"…but I suppose he's one of those men who love all and any, but behind closed doors, and then moves on."

Aidan winced. "And you're not?" Zeb's love life was openly chronicled and had been for years. He hadn't dated anyone for more than three months in all the time he'd been in the public eye.

Zeb stuck out his tongue again. "Honey, I've never closed a door in my life, not if I can get publicity out of it."

Aidan bit back a sharp reply. Zeb had climbed to the top of his profession with a combination of good looks, business savvy, and the ability to grab attention whatever he was doing. And he craved it too, unlike Aidan. So what was that uncertain thread underlying Zeb's banter tonight? "It sounds like H-G is okay with his life as it is," Aidan said.

"But without funds," Zeb said smartly, "there'll be no money to climb the Elgar, or whatever it's called, unless he can muster up some good publicity."

"So, where do you come into this?" Even as he said it, Aidan could feel a cold chill clutch at his gut. "*No*," he said quickly. He didn't know what the favor was that Zeb was about to ask—or why, or how—but he had a horrible feeling he wouldn't like it. "Whatever it is, no."

"*Ade*. The thing is—" Zeb took a careful breath. And when had he moved out of Aidan's brother-thumping range? "—I need you to go out with him."

"I—Sorry?" Aidan shook his head, trying to clear what he'd obviously misheard. "He doesn't even know me. Why would he want to date me?"

"He doesn't. Want to date you, that is."

Aidan blinked at Zeb's casual dismissal. "Thanks. I think?"

"No, I didn't mean that the way it sounded. Jesus, Ade, cut me some slack here." Another careful breath from Zeb. "He wants to date *me*."

"Does he know you?"

"No, of course not. You're the one who said we hardly move in the same circles."

Aidan stared at his twin. "Okay, so I'm now officially confused."

Zeb gave an exaggerated sigh and flopped back on the sofa. "It's a job. I do some work for his agency, and they need a gay date for Hairy Guy at a movie premiere next week. They've booked me."

Good God, am I on a completely different planet? He couldn't understand a word of it. "Why would they do that?"

For the first time, Zeb looked uncomfortable. "I do that sometimes. Go on a date with someone when the agency wants some publicity. They pay me a fee for it."

The paparazzi followed Zeb like faithful, lusty puppies when he went out in his full social regalia. But Aidan wasn't sure how to take this particular snippet of news. He knew Zeb went on dates enthusiastically and often—he'd just never imagined that anyone had hired him to do it.

Zeb went on grumpily. "Take that bloody look off your face. It's usually fun. It's just that this time…."

"Is going out with H-G so hideous a thought you want to pass him off onto me?" Aidan said icily.

Zeb rolled his eyes. "Please, bro. It's not like that. I'd do the gig, no problem. It's just I have to be somewhere else that night. But I'm under contract for the date as well."

"So you want me to date a complete stranger—and as you, not myself?" Aidan scoffed. "And what part of that do you think sounds likely?"

"Oh Ade, please." Zeb looked genuinely miserable. There was no sign of the wheedling look he'd had in the past when he tried to persuade Aidan to cover up some indiscretion.

"What aren't you telling me? I'm sure you've never passed up the chance of a date before. At least if you thought there might be a contract in it for you."

"Ouch." Zeb looked genuinely offended.

"And you've never been upset at comments like that before either," Aidan said slowly. What had changed with Zeb? "I reckon you've had a better offer and I'm getting your castoffs. Am I right?"

But Zeb didn't rise to the bait. He just looked more miserable. "I can't tell you any more. Not yet. But it'll really help me out. *Really*. I promise you this is genuine. It's no joke."

"But… a blind date?" Aidan couldn't get his head around it. "You know how I feel about those."

"Every date is blind until you get to know them."

"Don't quote platitudes at me, *bro*. This is ridiculous." Aidan had been on a totally blind date twice. Once he'd been abandoned in the middle of a town in Essex where the guy had received a call from his ex and rushed straight home—oh, and mistakenly took Aidan's wallet with him—and the second time, Aidan had narrowly missed being beaten up by a man who turned ugly after a few too many scotches. "And it's not because it's a blind date. It's because it's *me*."

"Ade." Zeb looked genuinely distressed. "I wouldn't even consider it if I thought you'd get into any trouble, honestly. Do you believe me?"

Unfortunately Aidan did.

"And it's just one evening. You probably won't even have to talk to him much. There'll be things going on—"

"*Things going on*?"

Zeb winced at Aidan's tone. "Just the premiere. And dinner. And then a couple of clubs, that's all."

Words failed Aidan. "*All.*"

"You're not dating at the moment, are you? I mean, you haven't got any commitments?"

It was Aidan's turn to wince. "Nice of you to ask first."

"Oh fuck it. I just make things worse and worse, don't I?"

And then Aidan just had to smile. "You look like a kicked puppy. No, I'm not dating anyone. But you do see how lunatic the idea is, don't you? I couldn't pretend to be you for an hour, let alone a whole evening. I mean, for a start, what would I wear? I don't have anything like a supermodel's wardrobe."

Damn it. He should never have started to talk logistics; he could see from Zeb's smirk that Zeb thought he'd won. As, of course, he probably had, but Aidan would make him work for it.

"I'd sort that out for you, you know I would. I can bring around a whole pile of outfits for you to choose from. And you wouldn't have to dye your hair or shave your eyebrows or anything—"

"Well, *that's* a relief," Aidan murmured sarcastically.

"—for just one night. We can make you look enough like me to get away with it."

Aidan shook his head. What more could he do? The plea in Zeb's eyes had been unmistakable.

"There's one bit of good news," Zeb added slyly. "You can have the fee."

Aidan felt a shameful mix of emotions. On the one hand, he really needed the money, and Zeb's fees always seemed obscenely huge for just standing around in ludicrous clothes all day. On the other hand, dating someone for money… didn't that make him some kind of a tart?

"I know," Zeb said in that fascinating way he had of knowing exactly what Aidan was thinking, "but I'm not asking you to put out. There's definitely no expectation of that. In fact, Hairy Guy—"

Zeb stopped suddenly as if realizing he was heading into more trouble.

Because, of course, Aidan had the same talent for knowing what his twin was thinking too. "He doesn't want to go on this date either, does he?"

Zeb sighed and struck what he called his *Les Miz* pose—a sad, plaintive look on his face and his hands lifted in front of him in supplication. "It's just a job for both of us, you know? Neither of us would have chosen it left to ourselves, would we? It's a necessary evil."

Way to make us all feel bargain basement. But that's what Aidan was nowadays, wasn't he? "What the hell would I talk about?"

"Honey, there's hardly any chance to talk at premieres anyway. It's just a matter of smiling and holding his arm. You know."

Aidan didn't, but he stayed silent.

"You did all those years at drama school, right? You move well from all the dancing you do with those hyperactive kids. And, let's face it, you know enough about my life to make small talk."

It was true. One thing Zeb loved to do when he was off duty was to talk. On many late nights, he'd come to visit Aidan and talk for hours about the people on the shoot, the director's instructions, the clothes, the client's instructions….

But I'm never the one in the spotlight. Aidan had realized early on in his acting studies that although he adored the theater, he was never going to make it as an actor. He couldn't lose his inhibitions convincingly enough. His stuttering and clumsiness onstage became legendary until no one in his class would cast him except in "stand at the back and don't speak" parts. And yet he was popular and had a beautiful speaking voice coupled with a deep love of language. Finally Aidan had found his niche in writing and directing and the occasional voiceover jobs—anything where he didn't have to be in front of an audience.

"And you do those commentaries and adverts, don't you?" Zeb was still rambling, his tone increasingly more panicked. "You can sound like me, no problem. You've always been the clever one, Ade. I need you to make this work for me. You never know, you might even enjoy it!"

Aidan thought that was about as likely as him joining the Royal Shakespeare Company, but one look at his distressed twin, and Aidan knew what answer he'd give.

Chapter Six

"DOM, stand still! I'm only going to trim this bit at the side, but if you keep wriggling I'm likely to stab you in the jaw."

Tanya stood on her tiptoes in the middle of Dominic Hartington-George's living room and snipped at the edges of his beard with nail scissors, fussing way too much in his opinion. At the same time, Eric hovered behind him, brushing the little ends of hair off the shoulders of his brand-new shirt—which was too tight, too bright, too stiff, too… *new*. Dom couldn't remember the last time he'd worn a smart shirt, let alone the whole new outfit that Tanya had bullied him into buying. He huffed out his frustration and Tanya leaned away from him with a frown.

"What's up, big man?" Eric kept up his usual teasing. "Nervous of a blind date?"

"Eric," Tanya warned.

"Don't be ridiculous," Dom snapped. But he *was* nervous. What the hell was that all about? He couldn't remember being nervous about anything since that time on K2 when a snowstorm blew up and he couldn't see six inches in front of his face. Even then, they'd all just hunkered down and dug in until the weather cleared. Could that strategy apply here as well? He was pretty sure dating wasn't comparable with mountaineering. Then he thought about the anticipation of this date and how it was causing adrenaline to spike through his body, and he wasn't so sure.

Dom had looked up this Zeb Z person online. Well, it'd been bloody hard to avoid him. Even as Dom typed in "Zeb," hundreds of searches and images sprang up. It had felt like a visual mugging. Dom didn't follow any particular magazines or TV channels, but even he recognized some of the campaigns Zeb had been featured in. In fact, he'd never realized how many of them were the same guy. Zeb Z had been the face of chewing gum, designer sunglasses, and diet soda, all within the same six-month period, though Dom found a glamorous swimwear campaign rather more fascinating. Zeb Z was one of those "pale and interesting chaps," as Dom's aristocratic mother was wont to call the more effete of Dom's friends. But Zeb had a finely developed set of muscles, a body that twisted both athletically and elegantly, and the most mischievous grin Dom had seen for a long time.

Well, even if they had nothing to say to each other, Dom thought he wouldn't mind a friendly grope of that body. He was mildly surprised to find his heartbeat had increased and his trousers tightened across his lap, just from admiring Zeb's half-naked body. A little too skinny for Dom's usual taste, but the chap's expression hinted he wasn't averse to some slap and tickle. Just for fun, of course. God forbid Dom would have anything more in common with such a media grabber. He'd found the occasional online interview with Zeb Z, and they seemed to be full of the clubs and parties he went to, the celebrities he'd met, and the stars he'd dated.

Slap and tickle? As if that were likely! Dom smiled ruefully at his own arrogance. Zeb Z was probably thinking the same thing at the moment, wondering what the hell he'd let himself in for, but without any desire to grope a grumpy, approaching forty-year-old in return. The kid looked all of twenty in most of his photos, even if Wikipedia insisted Zeb Z was twenty-eight.

"How's that?" Tanya waved a hand mirror in front of his face. She seemed to expect his feedback.

Dom didn't check himself out in mirrors as a matter of course, and it was a bit of a shock to see the smart man reflected back at him, with tidy hair, an ironed shirt collar, and his broad shoulders being eased into a new linen jacket by a smirking Eric.

Tanya sighed. "And *there*. You've just spoiled it with another scowl."

"Don't fuss, for God's sake." He tried to force a more relaxed look. "I'm fine. Honestly."

Tanya glanced at her watch. "He'll be here to meet you soon."

"The pair of you don't want us gooseberries lurking around," Eric said, following his words with a wicked little laugh.

Dom tried to grab him, but Eric had too many years' practice of keeping out of reach. "One day…," Dom threatened instead, "when you least expect it."

"Stop bickering, you two. But Eric's right, we'd better be off." Tanya picked up her bag and coat to leave the house.

"Tanya?"

She turned back to Dom, smiling distractedly. "What can I do for you?"

"I just want you to…."

"To…?" Tanya waved her hands helplessly as if trying to grasp an ending to that sentence from thin air.

"To come with me? To go on the date for me?" Dom only meant it as a joke, but Tanya flushed.

"I would if I could, Dom. He's really… you know."

No, Dom thought, *I don't*. Or maybe he did, but didn't want to admit it.

"He's very attractive. Bold." Tanya looked quite flushed. "And I believe he dates both men and women."

"An equal-opportunities man. Very modern." Dom's forehead crinkled as he tried to recall what he knew of Tanya outside work. "I thought you had a boyfriend?"

Tanya rolled her eyes, her usual practical attitude returning. "I have a husband and eight children, Dom. Thanks for remembering."

"God. You do? I mean, sorry I forg—"

Eric snorted.

"It's okay," Tanya said with a fonder smile. "I'm just teasing you, Dom. I only have a boyfriend, and no kids, though that doesn't mean I can't appreciate good-looking men, does it? But this is something you have to do for yourself."

"Well. Yes. Of course I do."

"You've dated before, right?" Eric sounded genuinely curious.

"God, yes. But… you know."

Apparently Tanya did. "With guys like yourself?" she asked shrewdly. "Strong, silent types who don't talk about their feelings, who just get on with the job? No strings attached, just passing relief?"

Dom winced. It sounded very grim, spoken aloud like that. "I'm not a complete tosser, Tanya. There have been men I've cared about."

"I'm sorry. I didn't mean to offend you."

"You didn't." Dom sighed and moved to run a hand through his hair, but he remembered at the last minute that he'd come away with a handful of gloop if he did. "In some ways you're right." Dom had dated men when he was younger and had hope, when it had been more than just relief and harmless fun. But nowadays? What time and emotional energy did he have for significant others?

Yet he seemed to be wearying of quickie hookups, as the kids called them. Sometimes he even found himself wondering about companionship and longer-term commitment. He had no idea why that was happening, apart from the Big Forty milestone approaching him in the fast lane. Being alone had never been a problem— dammit, he spent many months of the year away on walking and climbing trips, with no emotional hardship at all—but when he came home, it was different. The house was chilly and too quiet, there was nothing decent on the TV, and no one to complain to about it. Meals for one looked increasingly sparse and unappetizing. Was that what loneliness meant? Dom had no idea if it was a sign of age or weariness. He still had the same hunger for adventure—he just wanted something else as well.

But he had no idea how to change his "no strings and easy relief" approach to cope with that.

Tanya still looked concerned. "I thought it'd be a good idea for you to meet Zeb here before the premiere."

Dom hated the thought of pity, but he would always respect Tanya's intelligence. And to be honest, he found he suddenly welcomed her sympathy. "So we can vet each other? Check we don't throw up on the spot?"

Tanya started laughing, then bit it off. "You have an hour or so to chat before the event, and there'll be dinner and a club visit afterward. You don't want to arrive looking as if you've only just met, do you? Dom, please relax."

"I'm perfectly relaxed!"

"Yeah, right," Eric muttered from somewhere safe behind Tanya.

She's right about me, of course. Dom knew he was one of those men who didn't like to talk about their feelings. He relied on nature to provide the majesty and beauty in his life. What human could compete with that? "It means such a lot to me," he said suddenly. "This expedition. My father took the same route, you know?"

Tanya nodded, but she was obviously tactful enough to let him continue.

"I want to follow that route. *His* route."

"And conquer it," she said quietly. "I know."

He was silent for a moment. His father had been an amazing, charismatic, larger-than-life character, brimming with fierce energy and an iron will. And an appallingly negligent parent. Yet Dom had worshipped him as a kid, and he was still carrying that candle. Or was his determination to follow in his father's footsteps—and yes, Tanya was right, to cover them with his own imprint—a sign of rebellion against that reputation?

"We'll get the money, Dom." She took his arm gently. The touch broke him away from his memories. "Just play the game for a while, and then… well, then you can do whatever you wish. You'll be left on your own again, just as you like it."

Just as you like it. Dom couldn't blame anyone for thinking that was what he wanted. Meanwhile, he had a date to get through.

It would be one of the most challenging expeditions he'd ever undertaken.

Chapter Seven

BY the time Aidan arrived at the Hartington-George house, he was a whole new person—at least on the outside.

Zeb, of course, had loved rummaging through his own wardrobe to provide a whole set of alternative options for Aidan to wear. A few days after Zeb's bombshell announcement, he'd arrived at Aidan's flat with several cases of clothes, accessories, plus hair products to make Aidan's hair match Zeb's highlighted spikes. Aidan barely escaped wearing full makeup at the trying-on session; he refused anything beyond eyeliner and some tinted foundation. Although Zeb hated being out in the sun, Aidan was still naturally paler, but by the end of their time together, they looked extremely similar. To a cursory viewer, they could be the same person.

It was always fun to spend time with Zeb. Aidan just wished this time it had been for a less disturbing reason.

The pretty young woman who met Aidan at the door smiled warmly. "I'm Tanya, Mr. Hartington-George's personal assistant. I'm pleased to meet you, Mr. Z. I'm quite a fan."

"Zeb," Aidan said, hoping he hadn't hesitated for too long. "Please just call me Zeb. And… yes. Thanks."

"Come on through." She gestured him into the hallway. "You're on time."

Aidan wondered why she sounded surprised at that. He repitched his natural voice a little higher to Zeb's teasing tone and smiled brightly in return. "Of course."

A sneaked look in the hallway mirror had him rolling his eyes. *Mission accomplished, Zeb!*

He barely recognized himself. Usually he was most comfortable in a sweatshirt and jeans, but now he was dressed in what Zeb Z would wear on a daily basis: a pair of skintight, distressed-denim jeans with inexplicable splits across the knees; high-top boots in soft purple leather that screamed expensive yet were surprisingly comfortable; and two lightweight T-shirts under an off-the-shoulder, electric blue sweater. Admittedly the blue brought out the color of his eyes— no one ever said Zeb didn't have a well-developed sense of personal style—but the rest of it made him look like an over-age member of a boy band.

A younger man darted out from what must have been the living room, clutching a leather jacket to his chest as if in protection. He saw Aidan, glanced at

Tanya with widening eyes, then back at Aidan. Then he thrust out his hand and said perfectly cheerily, "I'm Eric. He threatens to kill me on a daily basis."

Aidan just shook hands and nodded. He had no idea what to say to that, or even what it meant.

Tanya frowned at Eric. "Whatever. We're just going. The car will come for you at seven. In the meantime, if you'd like a drink?"

But Eric took her arm and guided her toward the front door. "They can cope with that themselves, Tanya. Come on."

And Aidan was left on his own in the hallway.

He took a deep breath to center himself. The house wasn't huge, but it was in a very fashionable area of Ladbroke Grove and far more luxurious than his own small flat. That said, there wasn't much furniture and the decoration wasn't modern. The hallway walls were painted in plain, cool colors. No pictures hung on the walls, and there was only a single bureau and hat stand, albeit in quality wood. Eric had left the living room door ajar behind him, and Aidan took a quick peek inside before announcing himself. From what he could see, again the walls were plain and the furniture sparse. It was as if the owner was in the process of moving out—or had never really settled in.

A male figure paused in front of the half-open door. He was distracted by something on the other side of the room, so Aidan got a first secret glimpse of the man he'd been told so much about.

H-G.

He was much more handsome in real life than on TV, though in most of the documentaries, H-G was wrapped up in furry parkas or oilskins with his face more than half hidden with a scarf and balaclava. Today he was wearing a very smart pair of dark trousers, a startlingly white dress shirt—which had to be brand-new to still have that sheen—and a well-cut suit jacket that settled comfortably across an impressive set of shoulders. H-G's hair was a fabulous thatch of dark curls, and he had a dark beard and mustache to match. Guiltily Aidan recalled Zeb's mischievous nickname: Hairy Guy. But that conjured up a Wild Man of Borneo kind of image, and H-G was far from that. The hair was naturally unruly but had been styled to a level just off his shoulders, and the beard was well trimmed.

Aidan had never been attracted to hairy bears, not that he'd ever had much of a choice. As Zeb had gleefully pointed out more than once, Aidan seemed to attract needy and spiteful wankers who got off on bleeding him dry of any compassion and care. Oh, and his money too.

Okay. Self-pity over, right now. I'm not Loser Aidan now. I'm the charismatic and disgustingly fascinating Zeb Z.

For the first time in this bizarre performance, Aidan felt the tickle of mischief. This just might be fun after all. He pushed the door fully open, walked into the room, and cleared his throat.

H-G turned slowly around to face Aidan fully. His gaze ranged over Aidan's body, and his eyes widened. "Well. They didn't lie."

"Who didn't? What about?"

H-G raised his eyebrows. "Well, firstly, they said you were a bit feisty."

Feisty? Aidan hadn't heard that word outside of romance-novel blurbs.

"And you wouldn't be fazed by… you know."

"No, I don't know. By what?" Aidan bit his lip to stop a laugh escaping.

"My celebrity."

Jesus. Zeb was right. The man was one big blob of arrogance. "No," Aidan said coolly. "I'm not."

"That's from working in the business, I suppose."

"Business?" Oh, right, he was meant to be Zeb. "Yes, of course. When you've seen so many guys without the spray tan and makeup," he gabbled without thinking first, "you soon realize they've got the same equipment under it all."

H-G blinked twice, hard. And then he laughed—a loud, bold sound, echoing warmly in the bleak room.

Aidan wanted to laugh with him, but maintained his cool stare. "What's so funny?" Had he blown it already? He hadn't even left the house with the man yet.

"They didn't tell me you were witty, Zeb. I may call you Zeb?"

Why? "Oh yes, right. Of course."

Dom's language was quaintly old-fashioned, but Aidan found it rather charming, especially after the theatrical bickering of the Dreamweavers and his brother's exuberant and affected chatter.

"And secondly?" Aidan prompted.

"I'm sorry?" H-G frowned at him.

God, what a scowl he has. "You said they didn't lie, and then you gave the first reason."

H-G raised his eyebrows. "You have a good memory."

Yes, he does *have lovely eyes.* "Yes, I do. Especially when I'm listening."

H-G's mouth twisted as if he were trying not to smirk. "*Secondly*, they didn't lie about your looks, and that you were even better-looking in real life. I concur. You're bloody gorgeous."

Aidan wondered whom H-G was talking about. Zeb was the one who'd made a career based on his looks. Aidan made his on ignoring his own. So obviously H-G was talking about Zeb—or Aidan-as-Zeb. Aidan tugged self-consciously at the skintight jeans. His briefs felt uncomfortable between the cheeks of his arse and the hairs on his lower belly had snagged under the buttons of the fly. How the hell did Zeb manage to walk straight in these on a daily basis? "And you're bloody blunt," he returned smartly.

H-G tilted his head. He was smiling openly now as if he was enjoying the banter. "I've never seen any reason to be otherwise."

H-G's gaze didn't make Aidan entirely comfortable. "Like what you see?" he said rather too snappily.

But H-G just laughed again. "You're not as androgynous as you look in the magazines either."

"What does that mean?"

"You look all man to me." H-G's eyes darkened, and for a moment his gaze grazed over Aidan's groin area.

Aha! "So you've seen me in magazines?"

H-G flushed. "Now and then. Dentist's waiting room, you know?"

Aidan felt he'd scored a point there but wasn't sure how to follow up any advantage. This was turning into an odd kind of tennis match.

H-G cleared his throat. "Look, let's both be frank about this, okay? I know this is just a promotional exercise. The sponsor is very committed to equality issues, and to have a gay couple approaching them is apparently a good PR thing."

"You're doing this solely for the money?"

"Not to the extent of turning gay for it, no," H-G snapped back.

For the first time, Aidan saw a flicker of the real emotions inside the man. "Sorry. I didn't mean it that way."

"No, I'm the one who's sorry." H-G seemed to make a conscious effort to get his temper back under control. "I know you didn't. It's just one thing I never compromised on. I know who I am, what I feel, and what I like."

"That's good," Aidan said more gently. "I suppose you might have trouble with it sometimes."

H-G gave an angry shake of his head. "Anyone doesn't like who I am isn't worth being with. That's always worked for me."

Apart from having to hire a date for this evening. But then, Aidan didn't have a boyfriend either, did he? And he was the complete opposite to the aggressive H-G. Aidan didn't keep his sexuality hidden, but he didn't go broadcasting it around either. *Unlike my outrageous twin.* Could this outfit be any more obvious? The jeans squished his balls back and pushed his cock forward. The electric blue sweater had slipped off his shoulder again so that he felt like a provocative 1950s starlet, and it was itching his neck on the other side. It made his mood just as scratchy. He wondered briefly whose approach would be more successful in finding a soul mate—his, H-G's, or Zeb's.

"Anyway, mustn't forget my manners." H-G approached him and offered his hand. "Welcome to my home."

Aidan laughed softly and shook it. "Many thanks."

"And what about you?" H-G's voice still had a sharp edge.

"Sorry?"

"Have you had trouble with being gay? I suppose not, in the fashion business."

Aidan bit his lip. Yes, he'd had trouble. *Aidan* had had trouble: bullied at school, beaten up outside a bikers' pub one night in his teens, and as an adult, a bank official had openly sneered in his face and made comments about the poor credit rating of "party-going people like him." Aidan had lost several vacation jobs to less-qualified people, purely on the basis of their macho and/or more conservative looks. Even in his drama-school days, while playing out their early, often immature plays in the Student Union, there were occasions when audience members from the local community had seen the largely young and gay cast and walked straight back out. Did they think they'd catch something from the interval drinks? Didn't they want something more inclusive than TV soap operas? It had made him angry at the time, but he just shut up and got on with things. Until it got to the stage of one opening night too many, and Aidan withdrew from performing altogether, except with his pen.

He had much more control over that.

Gradually, that was the direction he'd taken his writing: toward that inclusivity, toward familiar scenes but with different gender dynamics. Despite any discrimination he'd suffered personally—or maybe, because of it—Aidan hated categorization of any kind. He often argued with Zeb about it, but Zeb laughed off everything that got too serious or personal, whether it was political, sexual, or just what he had for breakfast. For Zeb, maybe it was denial or fear: he'd been targeted at school the same way Aidan had, but Zeb's life nowadays seemed easy enough.

So maybe the problem was with Aidan himself. Wasn't that the whole bloody reason he was here today?

He just didn't seem able to stand up for himself in the big bad world outside.

Chapter Eight

"AH… Zeb? Are you still with me?"

"Sorry?" Aidan's attention had drifted. What had H-G asked? Oh yes, about having any trouble being gay. "No. No trouble really. Well, some." H-G was looking at him with eyebrows raised again, as if he thought Aidan was mentally challenged. "I'm—" What was the current popular phrase? *Complicated*? "—actually not keen on being categorized." First rule of lying, right? Keep it close to the truth.

H-G looked impressed. "Good. I can identify with that. And I'm glad you're used to dating men publicly. No point having photos taken of us canoodling when you're grimacing every time I lick your ear."

Aidan gulped again. Firstly because *canoodling* was another of those old-fashioned words he rarely heard nowadays, and secondly because… well, he hadn't really thought this through. "You're going to do that?"

H-G gave an embarrassed laugh. "I was joking. Sorry. They tell me I'm not brilliant at it."

Aidan had to smile. How could he resist, when the guy looked so uncomfortable? "You get a lot of that? Photographers on the heels of your private life?"

"Try my damnedest not to, that's why I don't—" H-G took a deep breath. When he continued, he sounded irritated. "Let's say I give 'em little enough to go on. It's the stereotype. They think I'm some tough wild man, a different species. They're always chasing interviews. A scoop, they call it, when there's actually nothing to find out."

Nothing? "Right."

"But it's not a fraction of the attention you get, I'd think." Now H-G looked bemused. "You're like the media's favorite playboy, aren't you?"

Yes, Aidan thought slowly, *Zeb is*.

"Anyway, do you want a drink?" H-G cast around the room as if uncertain where his own furniture was. "We've got an hour to kill before the car arrives. Tanya left some wine here somewhere."

Aidan calmly walked past him to fetch the bottle of red wine on a table by the window. Tanya had also set out two glasses and a small plate of olives and snack biscuits. Aidan poured the wine and gazed hungrily at the snacks.

Zeb had warned Aidan that at the premiere dinner, the food would be scarce and late in coming. "Eat what you can, when you can," Zeb had said. "If it matters to you, that is."

Aidan enjoyed his food; he wasn't apologizing for that. When did food *not* matter?

"Stupid," said a deep voice from very close beside him.

"What the hell?" Aidan nearly dropped the wine bottle, which would have been a pity as he could see it was really good quality, but he recovered himself in time. Abruptly he put it back on the table and whirled around.

"God. Sorry." H-G took a startled step backward. "You're a high-strung creature, aren't you?"

"Most people would be, hearing 'stupid' bellowed into their ear!"

"I didn't mean *you* were stupid."

"Really?"

H-G had the grace to look apologetic. "Sorry. Again. I meant the snack things. Stupid, silly little nibbles that do nothing but get stuck in your bloody teeth. I wanted her to put out some decent stuff for us to fill up on, especially when Eric said what crap the food is at these events. But Tanya, bless her heart, said you model types wouldn't want to see huge great plates of food."

"Huge great plates?" Aidan tried to damp down his wistfulness. He hadn't eaten much that day, what with the fuss of dressing up as Zeb, his nerves about the date, and the fact he'd run out of weekly grocery money and was waiting for an advance from Zeb's fee. "Decent stuff?"

"I've got cold roast beef in the fridge. Mustard, pickles, strong horseradish. Thick, fresh bread."

Aidan was mortified at the soft moan that might or might not have escaped his lips, but H-G seemed thoroughly pleased at his reaction. H-G's eyes were brighter than before, his manner more relaxed.

"Follow me, then. I've never been keen on this room. My mother decorated it, and her style's somewhere back there with the Edwardians. It's a damn sight warmer in the kitchen, and we can settle in properly."

IN the kitchen, Aidan sank gratefully into one of the wooden kitchen chairs without a second thought, and H-G seemed equally happy to avoid ceremony.

H-G had been right: the room was far more cheerful, with brightly colored tiles, modern fittings, and a haphazard scattering of utensils and ingredients on the counters that proved the owner cooked there regularly. They chatted about food they both liked—with plenty of shared enthusiasm—and TV chefs, and recipes, and some of the bizarre world foods H-G had eaten on his travels. Aidan fetched plates from the cupboard while H-G buttered the bread with a generous hand. A half hour passed very pleasantly before Aidan took stock of the situation, remembering the odd circumstances of being there at all.

He couldn't remember when he'd last tasted such good meat! And H-G didn't skimp with the bread and fillings. They both munched through a couple of rounds of sandwiches, then fruit and yogurt from the best-stocked fridge Aidan had seen in years. It was glorious to feel satisfied again—even if he had to slip open the top button of his jeans under cover of his sweater.

Right then H-G was preparing strong espressos from a coffee machine on the counter. It involved a couple of muttered curses and H-G thumping the side of the unit to get it going, but then it produced a fabulous aroma and steady drips into the coffee cups.

"So, where are you thinking of taking me?" H-G called over without turning around.

Aidan had been wondering whether the coffee machine was at fault or if it was operator error. H-G didn't seem to have a large reserve of patience. "You mean, after the premiere?" H-G turned to face him, and he had that "are you mentally challenged?" look again. "Oh, of course." What had Zeb suggested? "Maxima is our first stop. A new club, small, around the back of Soho, quiet—"

"Quiet?" H-G interrupted with a hopeful look on his face. He carried over the coffee with something approximating triumph. The china cups looked miniscule in his large, strong hands.

"Relatively so. But then we can move on to a couple of dance clubs." Aidan smiled slyly. "We should be seen in as many places as possible, having fun. This is a PR campaign, remember?"

H-G's expression was grim. "I don't."

"Don't what? Remember why we're here?"

"Dance. Don't dance." H-G looked truculent. Even the way he dropped back into his seat was vaguely antagonistic.

"Jesus. That's the last thing on my mind." But the mischief was still tingling in Aidan's veins. He wondered for one brief, wild moment what H-G would look like in the middle of a club dance floor, with that brand-new dress shirt peeled off and the sweat trickling down the hair between his nipples and over his abs....

"But that's not true," H-G said abruptly.

"Sorry?" Aidan was glad of the interruption to his startlingly carnal thoughts.

"About dancing being the last thing on your mind. You always dance. In all those interviews, you talk about the clubs and the music and the freedom of...." H-G paused and almost grimaced. "Letting your hair down." He stared unabashed at Aidan's spiked-up hair. "It looks longer than in the publicity shots they sent me."

Aidan ignored the fact H-G had obviously been swotting up on Zeb Z, and tried to salvage yet another slip in his performance. "Well, yes, of course I do. I love dancing." *Not.* Past boyfriends had likened him to a puppet with cut strings. "But I sort of assumed you'd want something less... energetic."

The relief on H-G's face was immediate, and Aidan reappraised the man. Maybe the arrogance wasn't so ingrained, after all.

"Wait." H-G frowned. "Is the age thing a problem to you?"

Spoke too soon. The conversation had moved back into minefield territory. "The age thing?"

"You think I'm too old for socializing at clubs. For dancing."

"Don't tell me what I think!" Aidan snapped without thinking first. "You're the one who said you don't dance. Age has nothing to do with it."

"No. No, I suppose not." H-G looked sullen but rueful. "I just keep cocking this up, don't I?"

Aidan took a long breath before replying to that. "No. You're fine. We're just very different people."

H-G also took his time replying. "Yes. Maybe." There was a weird tone to his voice, as if he wasn't entirely sure of himself.

The toot of a horn sounded outside the house, and then a knock on the front door.

"That'll be the driver," Aidan said, not without some relief. He stood, brushed down his sweater—which seemed to have a magnetic fascination for dust, threads, and breadcrumbs—and waved toward the door. "After you, H-G."

Aidan realized what he'd said a nanosecond too late to grab it back. He expected to hear the proverbial pin drop in the sudden silence.

"What was that?" H-G said slowly.

Oh Jesus! Where was Aidan's fertile imagination when he needed it? "I said… aching knees. Yes, that's it. 'After you, my *aching knees.*' From sitting on the same chair for too long." He tried to laugh carelessly, but it sounded more like a cackle. *Shut up, you're just making it worse!*

H-G stared for a fraction too long for Aidan to be sure he believed him. But H-G didn't call him on it. He just shrugged, picked up the jacket that he'd slung over the end of the kitchen counter, and led the way to the front hallway.

Chapter Nine

DOM was prepared to consider this date better than expected. For a start, Zeb was marvelous eye candy. Even the driver had turned to gaze when they approached the limo. While Dom was scowling at the bloody cost of a huge vehicle like that when he could have driven them to the cinema himself in his far more sensible SUV, the driver had smiled solely at Zeb. He looked as if he expected Zeb to speak to him, or at least flirt a little. After all, that was the impression Dom had of the model's reputation, and the driver seemed familiar with him, but Zeb had been surprisingly restrained. He'd allowed Dom to see him into the car, then waited quietly while Dom climbed in the other side.

Dom knew he was out of practice with the whole relationship thing, but no one could ever say he didn't appreciate a good-looking man. Of course, Zeb was a model and far too skinny, which was amazing as no one could mistake his healthy appetite in Dom's kitchen. Dom supposed models all suffered from anorexia or bulimia of some kind. He sneaked a side-glance at Zeb. The man looked healthy enough, though it was difficult to admire him closely under that ludicrously baggy sweater.

A tinge of pink appeared on Zeb's cheeks, as if he was aware of Dom's gaze. Dom hadn't expected him to be this modest either.

God, what *had* he expected? Dom had never met a bloke like Zeb in the whole of his life, and if he was truly honest, he didn't know how to behave with him. He cleared his throat. It sounded horribly noisy in the ultraquiet limo. "So, have you been busy recently? With… um, photoshoots and things?"

Zeb made a snorting noise in the back of his throat. "It's okay. You don't have to make small talk. Believe me, I don't want to chat all night about the supermodel world."

Even curiouser. In Dom's experience most media types wanted nothing more than to gabble on about themselves all the bloody time. "What exactly are you getting out of this, Zeb?"

"I'm sorry?"

"You heard me. I think we've both been blunt so far. If we're not making polite chatter, let's at least get everything out in the open."

Zeb made that odd noise again, but this time it may have been the result of a smothered laugh. He glanced quickly at the front of the limo, probably checking the privacy screen was pulled shut. "I'm hoping to have a nice evening with a charming man."

"Oh, I've read the script." Dom chuckled. "Me too. But otherwise?"

"It's contractual," Zeb said. "It's been arranged between our agents to get us both publicity."

He didn't sound enthusiastic about it. Dom looked at the lithe, beautiful, sparkly-dressed young man and then compared that image to Dom's own awkward appearance in his new, unfamiliar finery. "Beauty and the beast," he murmured.

"What? Of course not."

Had Dom meant Zeb to hear that? "Well, we're an ill-matched couple, aren't we? I don't see how anyone would think we're genuinely out together by choice."

"Listen, H-juh—I mean, Dominic. I can call you Dominic?"

"Whatever you like, as long as it's civil." Although no one actually called him Dominic nowadays, except for his mother.

"Right. Well, I think you'll find people going out with all types. That's if you took a look outside your front door now and then. And we're all basically the same underneath the clothes and the glamor, aren't we? As I said before. It's not wise to judge a book by its cover… or a man solely by his looks."

Dom appeared to have hit a hot button of Zeb's. He stared at the young man's rather stern expression until he felt his own tension ebb away. "You're right. Of course you are."

"I am," Zeb agreed. And then—there!—was the genuine smile Dom had last seen bestowed on him after a second round of roast beef sandwiches. "And I just made a pompous idiot of myself, didn't I?"

"No," Dom said, also smiling. "But we do seem to be bouncing back and forth between foe and…."

"Friend?"

Dom nodded. "Which actually sounds like a pretty normal first date to me."

Zeb's smile became more relaxed. "So, why don't you tell me what *you* want to get out of this. I gather it's funding for a new expedition? Is it the next step of your Hartington Hike project?"

"You know about that?" Dom couldn't remember when he'd last been so startled.

"Of course I do. There was a documentary series when you launched it. Your father climbed some of the most challenging peaks in the world and published it all in his memoirs. Now you intend to follow his route and climb all the same mountains, but this time with a camera rather than a notebook."

Dom just stared.

"What? You think I only watch reality shows?" Zeb was pink again. "I remember thinking what a lovely tribute it was, to say nothing of what a great show it'll make. The scenery will be spectacular, and it'll bring the challenge of the climbs to life far more vividly."

"Good Lord," Dom muttered. "You're either a frustrated moviemaker or… are you a climber?"

"Hardly." Zeb looked momentarily startled, but his follow-up smile was friendly. "Though I have done the Five Peaks challenge, just after I left university."

Another hit between the eyes. Dom managed to bite back his incredulous "You climbed the Five Peaks?" followed by the equally incredulous "You went to university?" just in time. He was beginning to think Zeb was right, that he should venture out into the world more often. The only supermodels Dom remembered hearing about had been virtually snatched from the cradle and weren't known for academic pursuits. He felt his gut roil at his narrow-minded, isolated view of people outside his circle.

God help him if the feelings weren't the beginnings of shame.

"Well, you're right. Again. Apparently I've worked through my pittance of an inheritance and now I need to raise enough for the final trip in the Hike schedule, an expedition up the Eiger. Tanya—my agent, PA, girl Friday, whatever—says a sponsorship deal is called for. I just turn up and do what I'm told in order to obtain it."

"I doubt that," Zeb said. "The bit about doing what you're told, that is."

Dom let out a gust of laughter. "Well, I won't say I went calmly to the slaughter."

"But she's right too. You have a wonderful ambition that should get better exposure. Imagine the combined project of your father's memoirs and your photos! That'll be attractive to plenty of commercial ventures. It can be a win-win situation."

"You sound like you know what you're talking about," Dom said a little slyly.

"So do you," Zeb snapped back. "You don't seem like a naive man to me. You must know you need to build financial relationships and play the media. It's not viable nowadays to fund events personally. Who has the money for that, apart from the Richard Bransons of the world?"

"Who indeed?" Dom said wryly, but he didn't feel as defensive as he usually felt when talking about his plans with accountants and agents. Zeb seemed to speak from the heart. He understood the nature of the Hartington Hike, while being brave enough to call Dom on his resistance to the workings of modern commerce.

"Of course, in my father's day it was all paid for by the family coffers."

"That's a bygone age now. You're your own man, not your father." Zeb's eyes widened and his mouth stuck in a shocked O shape. "Oh God, I'm sorry. That went way too far."

Dom was still assimilating it when the driver tapped on the screen and called, "We're here."

They'd pulled up at the carpeted area in front of the London cinema. The spectators were standing behind ropes, a blur of expectant faces shining under the photographers' lights. Everywhere around the entrance was packed tightly. Photographers leered at the car like poised birds of prey, and the loud, excited chatter seeped through the limo's closed windows.

"Bugger me," Dom said without thinking.

"Oh my God," Zeb breathed. He, too, was staring out the window.

Dom looked across at him in surprise. If he didn't know better, he would think Zeb was somewhere between horrified and scared. But the kid should be used to this kind of thing, shouldn't he? Dom refused most of his social invitations by default, but surely a supermodel got invited everywhere?

Impulsively, Dom reached over and grabbed Zeb's hand, interlocking their fingers. "Ready for showtime?" he asked firmly, trying to make his smile both determined and friendly—no mean feat.

Zeb blinked hard, then smiled back. His pressure on Dom's fingers relaxed. "Yes. Thanks."

It sounded like a genuinely sweet response, despite models being jumped-up, self-obsessed media flakes— well, apparently. Dom wasn't sure what was going on, but one thing he knew for sure, he'd be damned if he'd let the media scare him off. "Come on, then." He popped the lock on the car door, pushed it open, and clambered out. Zeb's hand was still clasped in his, which meant Dom almost hauled him out of the limo after him. But when he glanced back, Zeb was still smiling.

The paparazzi turned as one to face them, having just harried another celebrity couple all the way to the entrance. There was a brief moment of confusion while some people obviously tried to place Dom and failed— but no one had a problem with Zeb.

"Zeb! Zeb Z!"

"Will you be staying awake for this one, Zeb?"

"Who's your partner? Is this a new romance?"

Dom paused and turned to smile at a photographer, but from the way the young woman winced, he reckoned he hadn't managed to get his social face on properly.

Beside him, Zeb leaned forward into one of the long lenses. "You lot need to get a life," he said. "And not mine!" A few of the reporters laughed. "Now let us pass, or I'll miss out on the free popcorn."

Dom watched as Zeb allowed a couple more photos. He wondered if anyone had heard the slight tremor in Zeb's voice when he faced the reporters, or saw the tension across his shoulders as he posed. Maybe Dom was imagining it. Then Zeb glanced back at him, they nodded to each other, and together they made a smooth but speedy charge along the carpet and into the cinema.

Dom realized he'd been holding Zeb's hand the whole of the way.

Chapter Ten

THE film was appalling. That was the only decent word Dom could find to describe the two and a half hours of his life he would never get back. Some kind of meld of space opera and philosophical time travel that just exhausted him. He could appreciate a good moral message when he saw one, but this movie seemed to have collected a dozen of them, thrown them into one of those blenders Tanya used for her breakfast power drink, and then vomited out the results. Dom shifted uncomfortably on his seat. He'd been doing a lot of that in the last half hour.

Zeb was pressed up quite closely to Dom because the celebrity TV presenter on Zeb's other side was of a size that he needed at least one and a half seats for himself. At least Zeb had taken off that bloody sweater, thank God. He probably thought Dom hadn't noticed how itchy it made him, but Dom was glad Zeb saw no point in making Dom itch and suffer as well.

As Dom shifted again, Zeb whispered, "You okay?"

Dom took a quick glance at his date. Zeb looked smaller without his bulky coverings, although he still seemed to have a heap of T-shirts on. Dom could see the small hollow where Zeb's neck joined his torso. Smooth, pale skin, with the slightest shadow on his Adam's apple. It looked very... *lickable*. Dom swallowed, ashamed of his suddenly sexy thoughts. What was the matter with him?

"I'll just be a minute," he whispered back, though not so quietly that the stocky Portuguese celebrity chef on *his* other side didn't turn and frown at him.

"Okay," Zeb whispered back.

Had that been a brief second of panic on Zeb's face? Dom had to admit he wondered how Zeb had stuck the movie this long. Dom doubted that sitting still in the dark with a load of stuffed shirts for several hours was a usual night out for Zeb Z. It wasn't Dom's idea of fun either, for that matter.

But at least he could do something about it.

"ERIC?" Dom muttered into his phone.

"Why are you muttering, big man?"

"Because I'm trying not to be heard, you moron."

"There's a weird echo."

"I'm in the gents."

"Whoa, too much information!"

"It's the only quiet place I can find to call you," Dom growled. "Just send the limo back to the cinema, will you? I'll meet it around the back in ten minutes."

There was a brief silence. Then Eric gave a short, tight sigh. "Don't tell Tanya," Dom said. Had that sounded too much like a plea?

"You have to do the feedback thing." Eric's voice sounded strained. "After the movie. You have to smile and say it's the best thing you ever saw."

"It's unadulterated crap."

Dom knew he had an ally when Eric gave a sympathetic chuckle. "What about the dinner afterwards?"

"Mass catering," Dom said. "Warm wine."

Eric sighed again, but in solidarity this time. "And interminable speeches."

"So?"

Eric's voice relaxed into something conspiratorial. "You're on. But don't get caught, and don't say anything… you know. That way you talk to reporters."

Dom thought of Zeb's far more charming put-down outside the cinema, and accepted that Eric had a point. "Mouth shut, I promise. I just have to get out of here."

"And make sure they have *some* photos to go on, or the whole thing's off."

"Yeah, yeah, of course. *Now*, Eric?"

DOM wriggled back into his cinema seat without any real concession to the other watchers. In fact, he took no little satisfaction in standing heavily on the TV chef's foot as he went past him.

Zeb's eyes glimmered at him in the dim light. "I thought you might not come back," he whispered. "I wished I'd joined you."

Dom felt a ripple of relief inside. It wasn't as if he'd ever cared what people thought of his ruder behavior, but for some reason it was a treat to see Zeb on his side. "Tempted to leave early?"

Zeb bit at his lower lip in a rather charming, boyish way. "The film's pretty bad."

"Another hour to go," Dom said gleefully.

"No! Really?"

Dom had no idea, actually. He hadn't bothered reading up about the film before it started, and he didn't recognize any of the actors. But he liked that flicker of horror in Zeb's eyes.

"We're meant to see it through, then give feedback to the press," Zeb murmured. "That's how it goes."

"I see." Dom stretched out his legs, making sure to give the TV chef a gratuitous jab to the shin. "That photographer outside asked if you'd stay awake for this one. Aren't you a movie lover?"

"Of course I am." Zeb looked confused, but only for a second. "Oh. Well, yes. I may have fallen asleep in a few of these events."

"So, why don't we leave now?"

Zeb looked momentarily shocked, then wistful. "That's not the done thing."

Dom was prepared to leave on his own, even though he knew Tanya would be furious. But he wasn't running from Zeb's company, just the bloody awful film. He gave a low chuckle. "You were the one who said you didn't believe I do what I'm told. I've already told the driver to pull up around the corner." He slid his hand back into Zeb's and was encouraged when Zeb didn't pull back. "Are you coming?"

AIDAN felt both thrilled and guilty all mixed in together. He and H-G had sneaked out of the back of the cinema like teenagers trying to avoid paying. The limo had scooped them up without anyone seeing and taken them to the next step of the evening's entertainment. And who could have failed to see the gleam of mischief and satisfaction in H-G's eyes? He'd made Aidan his fellow conspirator—and Aidan had surrendered to it far too easily.

Now they were crammed together in a tiny leather-seated booth at Maxima, one of the hippest London clubs—or so Zeb often told Aidan. They'd swept through the waiting line of guests embarrassingly swiftly and then hurried to a vacant booth. The club staff had fussed over them, assuring them they were VIP guests, and *of course* they could rely on the management's support for total privacy.

Aidan sighed to himself. *Yeah, right.*

Zeb had told him enough stories about being pursued into the toilets by reporters and fans for Aidan to know how much that assurance was worth. There'd be a minimum-wage someone in the kitchen or behind the bar who would respond to a few notes slipped into a back pocket, enough to let a journalist in the back door of the club—to say nothing of his tame photographer.

But at that moment they were on their own, and Aidan had time to gather his wits. H-G was frowning at a waiter who'd brought them table snacks and was now offering to get him a multipage wine list. H-G just barked his order at the waiter, who looked uncertain whether to be impressed or irritated, but scurried away to get the drinks. Aidan knew he should have protested when H-G didn't even ask him what he wanted, but he decided to choose his battles wisely with his imperious date.

Aidan was still reeling from the gaffes he'd made this evening. That stupid, smart-arse comment in the limo about H-G's father had been so rude, and the way he'd answered back to the photographers! It was like something Zeb would say, so he, Aidan, had just said it. What on earth got into him? Then he'd followed that up with sneaking out of the premiere and the formal dinner... but hell, who wouldn't? The thought of sitting in a stuffy, packed room for yet more hours, with mediocre food and a million ways to slip up in his performance? Aidan had been more than relieved to skip it. Luckily he'd remembered Zeb telling him he regularly fell asleep at these movie events. Aidan could understand why. For a rare moment, he felt he and his numb bum were in perfect accord with his brother. The life of a supermodel seemed far from 24-7 glamor.

But he couldn't forget that the whole point was to be seen with H-G. The premiere opportunity had been cut short—not that Aidan was complaining—but there needed to be some public exposure this evening to fulfill the deal.

At a loud *pop* from a champagne cork, Aidan nearly jumped off his seat. He swiveled around to face H-G. A bottle of red wine and a bottle of champagne in an ice bucket had arrived at the table, plus a selection of crystal glasses. H-G poured out a large glass of the red with an unmistakable look of relief. Then he caught Aidan's eye.

"Red for you as well? It's not as good as the one we had at my flat, but it's the best they could do here. Or bubbly? That sounds more like your thing." He reached for the bottle in the bucket. "The management insisted we take it as well."

"Nothing, thanks." He ought to keep a clear head.

"Rubbish. We both need the support."

Aidan looked longingly at the champagne. The bottle was extremely chilled: a dribble of condensation ran down its side and he could smell the tart fruit of the drink inside.

H-G had already poured him a glass, and Aidan took a sip with relief. Not that he was any expert in champagne, but it tasted fabulous. H-G was now perusing the food menu, but from the scowl on his face, that didn't seem to bear up any better than the wines. Aidan sat back in his chair, gulping generously at his drink. There was a certain attraction in letting someone else take the burden of decisions, at least for a short while. Was this what Zeb experienced all the time? Being waited on, being fawned over, being—?

"Bugger it!" H-G fell awkwardly against him, his elbow catching Aidan in the ribs.

"Ouch!"

"Sorry. I was just reaching for the nuts."

"Uh—?"

"The bowl of peanuts. Bloody table's so small."

"It's okay. No, really." Aidan tried not to panic, but the lack of personal space was proving tricky to handle. The booth was just too small for two people who *didn't* want to climb into each other's laps. H-G looked apologetic, but his thigh was still squashed against Aidan's and his hand rested on Aidan's forearm.

"Look—" Aidan turned to H-G, who was so close they nearly bumped noses. "—let's just relax into this, okay? We're meant to be on a date. We're meant to like each other. So it's natural we'll touch and be close." He couldn't believe he was saying this, and with such confidence, as if he was the one in charge. As if it was business as usual for him. "I mean, if we wince every time we move, it's obvious we're not comfy together."

"I see," H-G said slowly. "Very sensible." As he righted himself, he lifted his arm and slipped it across Aidan's shoulders.

Oh... what?

Aidan swallowed an extra-large mouthful of the champagne. It would be churlish to push H-G off now, wouldn't it? A waiter filled their glasses again, and more snacks had arrived at the table. Aidan could feel the warmth of H-G's arm against his neck—when had he rolled up his sleeves? Soft hairs brushed Aidan's skin like feathers.

Aidan cleared his throat. "So tell me about the mountaineering."

H-G snorted through a mouthful of nachos. He'd already finished all the peanuts. "Don't be ridiculous. You're not interested."

"Listen"—Aidan heard a sharp edge to his voice that he rarely used in public—"I'm pretty sure I said this before. Don't tell me what I am or am not interested in."

H-G muttered something that might have been "highly strung." Clearly, he said, "You're a model."

"Yeah, amazing, isn't it?" A wave of angry defensiveness rose up in Aidan. This man was casting aspersions, if not on Aidan himself then on his twin. "Amazing that a model has a brain."

There was a stunned silence between them, and then H-G laughed out loud again. Whether he realized it or not, he tightened his arm around Aidan's shoulders. "I'm a jerk, aren't I? And rude as hell."

"Yes," Aidan agreed robustly. "And what's more, I think you should stop trying to make a virtue of it."

"Good God. You *are* feisty!"

Aidan opened his mouth to argue further, but all that came out was a bubble of a burp. For a second he froze, completely mortified.

H-G laughed even more loudly. "That's the champagne talking. I like its style." He lifted his free hand and gestured to the wait staff to bring another bottle. "You're right, of course," he said to Aidan, his voice softer. "And I admire you for standing up to me about it."

"Well, I'm in no position, really, to tell you how to act." Aidan wanted to say more, but he had to be careful; the champagne was still bubbling in his half-empty stomach. "I'm being presumptuous."

"Virtues, vices," H-G said wryly. "We've both got them. I'll try and curb mine this evening if you do the same for yours. Deal?"

"Deal." Aidan put his hand to his mouth. "But I need to get some proper food to balance the booze. And soon."

Chapter Eleven

FROM that moment, the tension lifted. When the waiter brought the fresh bottle of bubbly, H-G ordered pie and vegetables for them both.

Aidan tucked into it with gusto. He felt he hadn't eaten so well for months. His ultralow-priced meals for one got old quickly. After mopping up the gravy with a slice of the rather pretentious artisan bread provided on the side, he glanced across to find H-G had finished his meal and was grinning at him. "What's so amusing?"

"I'm trying to reconcile the emaciated model look with the lion's appetite, that's all."

Emaciated? "Are you saying I eat like a lion?"

H-G shrugged, still grinning. "I'm a rude jerk, remember?"

Aidan bit back a reply while the waiter cleared their plates, but H-G spoke again before Aidan could phrase a suitable comeback.

"Have you really done the Five Peaks?"

"Yes, though it was just after university, so a few years ago now." That was another slip, he suddenly realized, because Zeb had dropped out of uni as soon as a model agency discovered him. But maybe H-G wouldn't notice.

"Tell me about it." H-G had moved closer again.

"Your project is far more interesting."

"But I'm interested in yours," H-G said. "I'm bloody bored of myself."

Aidan peered at him with some suspicion. Was H-G already drunk? He looked like the kind of man who could manage his alcohol... but there was a mischievous twinkle in his eyes and he was definitely in Aidan's personal space. He had sneaked his arm back around Aidan's shoulders; though to a casual observer it could look like H-G was just resting it on the back of their seat.

For God's sake! Aidan could almost hear Zeb's voice. *How are you ever going to get a man if you don't let anyone get near enough to touch?*

Aidan had to admit that H-G's nearness was stimulating. They were both getting sweaty as the evening wore on, but H-G's smell wasn't offensive at all, just warm and very masculine through the thin fabric of his shirt. His body was bulky against Aidan's slimmer frame, but it felt muscular rather than soft, and H-G had fully fixed his attention on Aidan. When H-G was concentrating, his eyes were a very deep brown and his expression was truly engrossed. If he toned down the aggression and let people see this more genuine side of him more often, they wouldn't think he was such a brute.

Aidan cleared his suddenly tight throat. "Well. It was a sponsored event, run through the Student Union. Only a few of us lasted through the training, but between us we raised thousands of pounds for a children's cancer charity."

H-G nodded approvingly. He grazed his fingertips against the back of Aidan's neck.

Does he expect more detail? Aidan described the journey for a few more minutes. He was pleasantly surprised to find that with H-G's encouragement and interest, the memories flooded back: the happy camaraderie, the sense of achievement, the heartfelt gratitude expressed by the charity they'd supported. He took a gulp of his champagne—the glass had miraculously refilled while he'd been eating—and launched into the raw truth. "To be honest, I suffered with hideous blisters on my feet. The climbing down was even harder than climbing up. And for weeks afterward, my muscles knotted every morning when I woke."

"Insufficient warm-up and -down," H-G said knowingly. "Regular massage would have sorted that out." For a brief moment, his other hand hovered over Aidan's thigh, then fell back to his side.

"You must train for months for the major climbs."

H-G chuckled. His drinking was keeping pace with Aidan's, but he didn't look any the worse for it. "You mean train all the bloody time. I never stop. I don't have any time for the other nonsense of life. It's my job, isn't it?"

"You're on a mission." Aidan smiled at him. "Tell me more."

And H-G did. He didn't go into a lot of detail, which made Aidan suspect he rarely found anyone to listen at length, but he gave brief histories of his last two expeditions. Even with the physical struggles played down and the anecdotes obviously chosen for Aidan's entertainment, Aidan was transported onto each trip with him. He found himself asking far too many questions about the equipment required, the planning cycles, the team that H-G had brought together each time. But H-G answered readily and expansively.

"How many times have you been to Nepal?" Aidan was particularly fascinated with H-G's recent climb of Makalu. "I'd love to see that part of the world. How did it feel to be thousands of meters above sea level?"

"Eight point two," H-G murmured.

"To take pictures of that as a beautiful, forever memory of the climb? To see the whole country laid out below you," Aidan continued excitedly, "rather than be down on the ground with everyone else?"

H-G looked bemused, and Aidan wondered if he'd said something wrong, but H-G answered his question. "It's brilliant. Almost indescribable. The scene is magical—if I believed in that stuff. To see the two snowcapped subsidiary peaks, the knife-edge ridges stretching across the range. It's the closest I've ever got to spirituality." H-G's gaze searched Aidan's face. He still looked confused.

"It must feel almost like you never wanted to come back down."

"Yes. Exactly like that," H-G said so softly that Aidan barely heard it.

Silence fell for a long moment.

Aidan stared back at H-G, seeking the truth behind the man's words. It was there, in H-G's bright eyes and suspiciously damp lashes, in the momentary disappearance of his habitual scowl, and in the catch of his breath, for his broad chest was barely moving. Aidan's own chest twisted uncomfortably and his heartbeat sped up.

"But that wasn't going to happen." H-G broke the spell with a more familiar gruff comment. "Got a call from the bloody bank. Amazing they can track you down in the middle of the bloody Himalayas, isn't it? The trip had run out of money, and I was summoned home to renegotiate the loan. Had to borrow most of the fare home from a mate. And so—" He lifted his free hand in a gesture of frustration, brushing right across Aidan's hip on its way. "—here I am today."

"But I assume that commitment comes with the territory. A dedicated explorer will be dedicated in all areas, whether it's the climb, the photographic record, or the finance. I suspect your father was as single-minded."

H-G's smile wavered. "More so. Climbing was all he ate, slept, talked, and dreamed." There was a thread of bitterness underlying the more obvious pride. "He wasn't interested in following anyone else's achievements or seeking the most famous mountains. He chose what he wanted to do, where he wanted to go. And then he did it in the fastest or most challenging way he could. It was all about victory to him and always on his terms. He was in one of the first teams to scale Makalu by the difficult west face. It was his penultimate climb."

"I'm sorry. He died…?"

"Three years ago."

"A hard act to follow?" Aidan kept his voice low.

"Bloody impossible!" H-G announced. A bit too loudly, in Aidan's opinion, because more than a few of the guests turned to stare. "I'll tell you the truth, Zeb, shall I?"

"If you want—"

The question was obviously rhetorical, because H-G had continued regardless. "He was a bloody awful father. He was hardly ever home, and when he was, he argued with my mother all hours of the day and night, then spent any free time in his study, planning the next trip or scarpering off to Wales or Scotland to put in the practice." He looked at Aidan; his eyes were a bit hazy. "The rock in both places is similar to some overseas mountain ranges, you know? But he always seemed to choose an inopportune moment for Mother and me to accompany him, so we were left behind again and again. It was his life, his time, he said. For God's sake, it was *all* his time."

"Please." Instinctively, Aidan put his hand on H-G's. "That doesn't mean you don't love him. Don't miss him."

The noise that came from H-G was an honest-to-goodness growl. "Why don't you call me by my name?"

"I—what?"

"You've barely mentioned my name in all the hours we've been here. Maybe you've forgotten it."

"Of course not." Aidan was just trying *really* hard not to slip up with H-G again. It had been so difficult to look at his date and see *Dominic*, not *H-G*. At least... it had been. Maybe not so much now. He risked another look into Dominic's eyes. "Hello, Dominic."

"Well hello, Zeb." Dominic's voice had gentled. "Sounds good in your voice. My name, that is."

Aidan was treading water here, trying to keep up with Dominic's mood. The moment of crisis seemed to be passing, yet Dominic was still tense. Aidan could feel it in his shoulder, where Dominic still grasped him.

"That's enough soul-searching, okay?" Dominic's eyes held a plea.

"Of course." Aidan would have apologized for taking the conversation into emotional territory, but that would probably only prolong it.

"And what about *your* family, Zeb? Not as dysfunctional as mine, I'll bet."

Dominic's smile was a bit of a grimace, but he was obviously trying for a lighter touch. He ran his hand back through his wavy hair, disturbing the careful style. Aidan watched the movement, liking the more natural look.

"I don't know about that." Aidan had been an orphan since the age of fifteen, when his parents were killed in a car crash. He and Zeb—or Sean, as he was in those days—had been taken in by a distant aunt and uncle, but it was only seen as a temporary measure until the pair of them could be self-sufficient. It had been Aidan who kept a hold on his grieving twin during those last few years of childhood. They were both distraught, of course, but Zeb was already volatile at that age and determined to go his own way. Authority and he became sworn enemies. His schooling had suffered; he'd barely passed any exams even though he was smart enough, and his halfhearted attempt at going to uni had ended in dropping out after three months to join a model agency. Whereas Aidan had worked doubly hard to get good academic results, kept an eye on the worst of Zeb's excesses, and made sure Zeb was taken in by a decent agent who would find him a place to live and give him good financial advice for his new riches.

Zeb was far more settled nowadays and had returned the favor a hundredfold, helping Aidan buy his own flat and trying to be there for him when needed. But… Zeb was Zeb. They'd always be as close as twins could be, but as two halves of the one whole, rather than the same personality.

And so… what more could Aidan tell Dominic about his family? He kept quiet, hoping Dom would drop the topic. No one even knew Zeb Z had a brother, let alone a twin. Aidan had lost track of the things Zeb had told interviewers over the years. Yes, that he was an orphan, but Aidan knew Zeb was infamous for making up entertaining stories rather than telling the bald truth, especially when it came to his past. The media forgave him anything and everything because he charmed them so thoroughly, and Zeb's newsworthy dates distracted everyone from digging into his family story. It was a clever strategy, but it didn't help Aidan now.

Oh, to hell with Zeb!

For the first time, Aidan actually found this whole project very empowering: being looked at in public, being perceived as a celebrity, being asked his opinion on things. Perhaps he should have been an actor after all, rather than always behind the scenes.

No! His mind swiftly contradicted him. The sudden thought of stepping onto a stage and facing a sea of blurred but expectant faces brought on a near panic attack. Public exposure was Zeb's line of work.

Yet, strangely enough, Aidan was coping well enough with it tonight.

Chapter Twelve

"I'M prying." Dominic gave a deep sigh and his breath rippled over the hairs on Aidan's neck. "You can tell me to get lost. Most people do."

The misery in H-G's—Dominic's—tone was uncharacteristic, at least as far as Aidan had come to expect. One of the things Aidan had enjoyed most tonight was the sanction to spend time with Dominic. To go out with an intriguing man without any of the usual worries of a first date. Obviously there were other tensions from this bizarre arrangement, but there was no commitment to meet again after tonight, was there? No pressure, apart from Aidan remembering his lines, such as they were. No need to get involved in small talk, to learn more about his companion, except what he was truly interested in. None of the paralyzing, emotional nervousness that usually tripped him up and made him act like a complete idiot.

Yes, he could just sit here, pretend to be his famous brother, drink, eat expensive refreshments, and ogle a very handsome fellow celebrity.

And be paid for it.

Aidan conveniently ignored that thought. He wasn't only doing it for the money; he was doing it to help out that famous brother. As he always did. No one was in danger, and no one would be harmed by a little light deception. He swallowed a generous half glass of his champagne and only vaguely wondered why the overall level in the bottle didn't seem to go down.

Of whichever bottle it was.

Aidan's body felt the warning signs of champagne and closeness to a handsome man long before his brain told him to take notice—the brain that was obviously taking a break somewhere else. He leaned into Dominic and put his hand on Dominic's thigh. Dominic's muscles seemed tense there, though that might have been because he startled at Aidan's touch.

"I know you didn't want to do this," Aidan murmured.

"What?"

The music was louder than when they'd arrived. Maxima was more club than restaurant and someone had upped the volume, but Aidan had no problem hearing Dominic over the background music.

"Go on this date. Be with me." Aidan felt the devil rise up in him. "You said it yourself: we're not much of a match. I expect your usual partners are far more impressed with your credentials."

"My… what the hell?" Dominic looked genuinely surprised. "I don't know what you're on about, but I don't set out looking for someone to impress. I want someone who's good company, a strong character. Who'll give as good as he gets."

Aidan couldn't help the wash of pleasure he felt at the indirect compliment. "No. I meant... well, you probably date bears like yourself, usually."

"Bears?"

Shit. Aidan knew he'd slid onto thin ice, but his stupid tongue wouldn't stop blabbing. "Sorry. I just meant tough guys like yourself. Big. Burly." Could he sink any further into the pit he was digging?

But it seemed to have broken Dominic's introspective mood. He started to laugh uproariously. "Burly? Does that mean you think I'm hairy too?"

H-G. No! *Dominic!* Aidan gulped. What was he meant to say to that after he'd been sitting there, peeking at the dark hairs curling over the neckline of Dominic's shirt, wondering how far down the rest of it went? Whether Dominic's legs were as deliciously furred, whether there'd be a decent treasure trail down to his groin that a man could tangle his fingers and nuzzle his nose into, to smell the sweet warmth of male skin....

Hairy skin. Strong arms. Warm, muscular thighs. *Oh fuck.*

The goose bumps ran over every inch of Aidan's skin.

"I *am* hairy, can't deny it. You like that idea?" Dominic's voice was low and growly. He couldn't have failed to notice Aidan's sucked-in breath, the tensing of his stomach muscles. "Do you want to check out my hairy credentials?"

Aidan stared at him. Was that a joke? Was Dominic really attracted to him? Aidan had never found his build much of an advantage. Yes, he and Zeb were blessed with excellent bone structure, and in Zeb's case the

grace of a dancer, but out in the bars and clubs Aidan
always seemed to blend into the background.

Ah, but he was meant to be *Zeb* now, wasn't he?

"I think you've misjudged me, Zeb." Dominic's
voice was very close to Aidan's ear now. He'd placed
his hand over Aidan's, pressing Aidan's palm onto
Dominic's thigh.

"I—what do you mean?"

"I wouldn't have thought you were my type, I
admit. But there's a spark between us, isn't there?"

Oh God, yes. But Aidan couldn't admit that, could
he? He gulped, wishing he'd eaten *three* pies, if only
to soak up the effect of the champagne. The warm,
heady excitement from his newfound courage wasn't
as robust as he'd thought.

Dominic smelled really good: a mix of vanilla
aftershave, or maybe just soap, and a breath of tannin
from the wine. Aidan couldn't help it; his lips opened
slightly and his tongue slipped out to moisten them.

"Dear Christ in heaven," Dominic said on a ragged
sigh. "You're really gorgeous." He sounded shocked.
Aidan remembered him saying it when they met at
Dominic's house, but now there was an extra rumble
underlying his voice. "Say my name again. I like it.
Most people call me Dom."

"Dom… Dominic." Aidan heard the words but
barely registered speaking them aloud. He was fixated
on Dominic's mouth, not his own.

Their lips touched.

Aidan gasped. It was the lightest of touches, but
like the heaviest bolt from the blue. It was as if Dominic
had breathed a flame into him through his mouth. His
whole body shivered with excitement, a trickle of pure,
heated delight on his skin compared to the sweaty air

of the club. Dominic rested his hand lightly on Aidan's shoulder, at the junction with his neck. He slid his fingers to the front of Aidan's throat and stroked the hollow under his Adam's apple.

It's not enough! Aidan wanted Dominic to slide his hand down under the T-shirts—remind him why he was wearing so many, none of which actually fitted properly?—and touch his skin. Properly, firmly, with need.

With a soft moan of pleasure, Dominic leaned in to take the kiss deeper.

Aidan responded very, very willingly. He slid his outer arm around Dominic's waist and pulled them closer together. Dominic lifted his other hand away from Aidan's and rested it on Aidan's knee. Their lower halves were hidden by the table, and Dominic's knee pressed very tightly against Aidan's. His large hand squeezed gently, and then slowly, teasingly slid up between Aidan's thighs. He nudged harder, trying to push Aidan's legs farther apart.

Aidan's head was swimming from the kisses. Dominic's mouth was still on his, his surprisingly soft beard rubbing along Aidan's jawline, his breath quickening. When Aidan twisted to get even closer, he felt the heat from Dominic's groin and Dominic's solid erection against his hip. He wanted to climb onto his date's lap, however ridiculous or rash that seemed. Instead he ran his free hand behind Dominic's neck and leaned in, excited despite himself at making out in a semipublic club. Dominic had cupped Aidan's cock and balls, trapped inside Zeb's skintight jeans. Now Aidan was aroused too; the seam of the jeans was pressing against his flesh, causing a strange, awkward, intoxicating pain. He half closed his eyes, relaxing into the embrace, enjoying Dominic's firm caresses under cover of the table. It had been a long time since Aidan did anything like this, a long time since he'd *wanted* to do it, in fact.

He wanted more, needed more. *Ached* for more—

And that was the exact moment a camera flash went off in his face.

What the hell? Sudden panic rose up as a lump in his throat and a double-time heartbeat. *What's happening?*

"Zeb?"

"Zeb Z! This way!"

Voices near the booth were loud and excited. Other diners turned to stare at the sudden action. Dominic let out an angry exclamation and gestured to the security men over by the bar.

Aidan's panic continued unabated. They were being invaded! A young man with gelled hair and greedy eyes pushed rudely onto the seat beside Dominic, and two photographers snapped Aidan from the other side. He wriggled away from Dominic, desperate to get away from the reporter.

Dominic caught his arm as he tried to slide out of the booth. "Zeb? What's up?"

"Let go," he said through gritted teeth.

Dominic started to laugh, then stopped when he caught the serious tone behind Aidan's words. "What the hell are you scared of? It's just the bloody press. Parasites, I know, just like outside the cinema. But we'll get rid of them—"

"No. I'm going. This is—" *Terrifying? Gross?* He couldn't even think straight.

"But this is what it's all about, isn't it?"

"No, it bloody well isn't. Not for me." He pushed Dominic's hand off his arm. "And I said let *go*! I'm not one of your bloody mountains you think you can... scale. Climb. Conquer!" He was a playwright, a wordsmith, for God's sake, but he couldn't seem to form coherent sentences.

Dominic looked as shocked as if he'd been slapped. "I thought you liked it. You acted as if you did. I thought it was part of the fun."

"You thought wrong," Aidan snapped.

"No, kid. I think *you* did." Dom's expression was thunderous now.

"And don't call me a kid!"

"Should I call you a cocktease instead?" Dom snarled.

Aidan was struck speechless. How could things have gone from so good to so bad, so quickly? The security men were bundling the reporter's team toward the exit and the manager was at their table, all but weeping his regret for the intrusion. But as far as Aidan was concerned, the damage had been done. People still stared at them openly, and he'd still been snapped with his tongue nearly down Dominic's throat. Where was all his newfound confidence? The pleasure from Dominic's touch? The warmth from being with a man he was really starting to like?

Gone.

Aidan scrambled out of the booth with less dignity than he would have liked, and surreptitiously adjusted the front of his jeans as best he could. He didn't meet Dominic's eyes or listen to the manager's apology. His objective was the exit, and as fast as possible. "I'm going home," he said.

He knew no one—not even Dominic Hartington-George—would argue with *that* tone.

Chapter Thirteen

DOM was feeling slightly stunned, and that wasn't only because it was eight in the morning. He'd hardly slept all night, and a near-hysterical Eric was on the other end of his house phone.

"What the hell happened, Dom? Tanya's going to go nuts. It's all over Twitter!"

"What is, exactly?"

Eric gave one of his snorts. He didn't bother to hide his true opinions from Dom, as Tanya so valiantly did. "There's a full color photo in the *Celebrity Exposed* feed of you and Zeb Z snogging in that bar—"

"Snogging?"

Eric didn't pause. "—then one of him rearing back from you in horror—"

"Horror?"

"Well, alarm, definitely. Then in the next shot he's up and away, charging into the photographer's lens like a mad thing, nostrils flaring, mouth open and spewing obscenities—"

"*Stop*!" Dom put every ounce of assertiveness into the word. He reckoned he could hear Eric wince even if he couldn't see it.

There was a long moment of silence.

"Sorry, Dom," Eric said eventually, more timidly.

"There were no obscenities," Dom said firmly. "At least not from Zeb. He was just startled."

"Yes, Dom."

Dom suddenly registered a buzzing noise on his desk, coming from somewhere under a couple of unfolded maps, a catalog of expensive outdoor goods, and a dirty mug from a previous day's morning coffee. That was probably where he'd left his phone. It rang persistently for another thirty seconds, then mercifully stopped. Dom didn't need to find it to guess Tanya was calling him. "Don't they say all publicity is good publicity?"

Eric cleared his throat. "Oh yes, yes. *Usually*. But this isn't necessarily the publicity we were... you know... hoping for."

Dom sighed aloud. It hadn't necessarily been what he was hoping for either.

"Dom?"

"Leave it to me, kid."

"Tanya will be getting in touch—"

"I said leave it to me!" Dom barked.

He clearly heard the sharp intake of breath on the other end of the line, even though Eric should be well used to Dom's ways by now. Dom couldn't help worrying; had he scared Zeb like that? He didn't have time to dwell on it. He finished the call with Eric.

His phone had started buzzing again. One day he would program it with different—and more palatable—tones for each of his contacts. Not that there was much point when he only accepted calls from his expedition buddies and Tanya.

Mr. Antisocial, that's me.

By the time he'd bundled all the wreckage off his desk, found his phone, and snatched it up to take the call, he'd had time to marshal his thoughts. "I know what you're going to say," he said preemptively.

"Unusually perceptive of you, Dom," Tanya's voice said wryly.

"I cocked it up." Tanya's startled gasp in reply was surprising, but Dom supposed she didn't hear those words from him very often. "You'll have to think of something else to improve my public profile and tempt the money in."

Tanya was silent. Dom wondered if they'd been cut off, but when she started talking again, he wished they *had* been.

"That's not possible at the moment, Dom. You need to see Zeb Z again."

"After that bloody impromptu photoshoot at the club?"

Tanya's voice held a thread of amusement. "That bloody impromptu, *high-profile* photoshoot, you mean?"

Dammit. "I thought, from the tone of Eric's panic, it would all be off by now."

"I know. But I've spoken to the sponsor, and they're actually intrigued. I don't think they'd have been convinced by staged photos and an attraction that wasn't genuine."

"You think?" Dom muttered, rolling his eyes for his own gratification, but Tanya either didn't hear his reply or chose not to rise to the bait.

"The pictures make you two out to be a couple with the normal kind of problems we all have. Trying to have a private night out, enjoying each other's company, showing affection."

"Look, about that kiss—"

"Then there are sometimes misunderstandings, arguments—"

Yes, yes, didn't I just say "about the kiss?" "Oh for God's sake."

Tanya chuckled. "Just take it easy, Dom, will you? Give the plan a chance. Give the young man a chance."

"What does that mean?"

"If he upset you somehow—"

"Oh hell no. It wasn't like that at all. Quite the bloody opposite." None of it was Zeb's fault, but what could he tell Tanya without sounding like a predatory monster? *I treated him like a piece of meat. I kissed him like I was falling down a crevasse and he was the only one with a rope. I groped him, thinking he'd be up for a cheap, quick fumble under the table of a public place.*

"Dom, what actually happened?"

"That's our business. I certainly don't want to talk about it." Not about the fact that Dom had scared off an unexpectedly attractive and intelligent young man; that he'd actually been enjoying the evening until that point; that Zeb had felt completely comfortable in his arms, his cheeky responses and natural charm completely blindsiding Dom; nor that the memory of Zeb's mouth had kept Dom awake for hours, reliving the touch. "Tanya?"

"I'm still here." Her voice sounded almost kind. "Let's talk over a plan. Come into the office today."

"No bloody way." Then he realized how graceless that sounded. "Leave it all to me," he added. "I'll sort things out. But I can't guarantee he'll want to see me again."

"Like you said, Dom, that's your business. Yours and Zeb's. And you know what's at stake. I know it's safe in your capable hands."

After she'd finished the call, he stood there for a few moments in the middle of the room, staring at the silent phone. Safe in his capable hands?

He'd never felt less sure of that in his life.

THE bells were ringing. And *ringing*. Aidan stirred under his duvet but didn't want to open his eyes. There was some kind of harmony going on, except the bells didn't sound properly synchronized. It was a painful sound. Several of them, in fact. Now a thumping beat had started up to accompany the bells. Except it didn't. It hammered its own tune, and Aidan wished it would just shut the f—

He lurched up in bed, his head reeling, his eyes still half glued together with sleep. What was going on? The morning light streamed in through his bedroom curtains; he'd obviously forgotten to close them last night. What time was it? And what were the chances of both his landline and his mobile phone ringing at the same time *as well as* someone knocking furiously on his front door?

He scrambled out of bed and quickly pulled on his sweats and a T-shirt. His head felt two sizes too big and his mouth was so dry he couldn't even feel his tongue. How much had he drunk last night?

Last night....

No. He wasn't going to think about it, not just yet. He stumbled along the hallway to his front door and yanked it open. Titus filled the doorframe like a human shield. "Morning, Shakespeare," he boomed.

Aidan winced. "You're.... Do we have a rehearsal or something?"

Titus's eyes narrowed. "No. I decided to call in on you because of the other night when you were so bloody miserable."

"I wasn't."

"Bloody was." Titus didn't wait for another protest or an invitation to come in, and pushed past Aidan into the flat. "I'll make us both coffee, though it looks like you need it most. Do you know all your phones are ringing?"

"Make yourself at home." Aidan wished he had the energy to put more sarcasm in it. Oblivious to it anyway, Titus pottered into the kitchen and started gathering the stuff to make drinks. Aidan snatched up the home phone. "Hello?" he snapped.

"Whoa! Hi, bro. Did I wake you?"

Zeb. "Sorry. No, I'm up and about." Aidan bit back a sigh. Was Zeb calling for a full postmortem of last night? Aidan wasn't sure how robust he felt at the moment, but it was good to hear his twin's voice. "Hang on... my mobile's going as well."

He grabbed for the other phone he'd apparently just slung on the couch, and peered at the incoming number. He didn't recognize it as anyone he knew. The phone stopped buzzing and then beeped with a text. Aidan opened it, fully expecting it'd be someone trying to sell him insurance or investigate his nonexistent car accident.

This is Dom. We have to talk. Call me back ASAP. Dammit. Typing is crap. Meant to start with please. Please call.

"Bloody hell," Aidan said.

"Ade? What's up? What did I say?" came Zeb's voice in his ear.

"No. It's not you." Aidan dropped onto the couch and ran his hand over his face. He'd shaved closely last night for the date and his morning stubble was only a light scrape on his palm. "How are things with you?"

"More to the point, how are things with *you*? How did the date go with H-G?"

"Oh, *marvelous*." Aidan stressed the sarcasm more this time.

This is Dom. We have to talk.

Titus strode into the living room carrying two mugs of steaming coffee. He clunked Aidan's down on the table beside the sofa, then settled himself in the armchair opposite. He gazed at Aidan with a curious and determined look. Apparently he was staying for a while.

Aidan sighed.

On the other end of the phone, Zeb gave a snort of frustration. "Ade, were there problems? Did they guess it wasn't me?"

"No, that all went fine. I'm all set to hand over to you."

"You're all set… sorry?"

Aidan glanced over at Titus, who was still shamelessly eavesdropping. "I can't go into details right now, but I assume you'll take the… *project*… from here on in. It was just the one night, after all."

There was a suspiciously worrying silence on the line.

Titus leaned forward and tapped Aidan's coffee mug. "I put extra sugar in," he said in one of his outrageously loud stage whispers. "Good for shock. Hangovers. One-night stands." He gave an equally outrageous wink.

"First of all, tell me what happened on the date," Zeb said in Aidan's ear.

"I can't." Aidan glared at Titus as if that would make the actor finish his coffee and go. Titus just smiled back. *For God's sake....* Aidan covered the phone with his hand and spoke to Titus. "This is personal. Do you mind giving me some privacy?"

"No problem," Titus said cheerfully. "I'll go and rustle up some brunch for us."

"What?" *Brunch?* Why didn't Titus just go home? And Aidan didn't think his stomach would appreciate food yet, but he decided it was easier just to go with the flow. At least it would get Titus out of the room.

As soon as Titus had left, whistling something Aidan thought was from *Oklahoma!*, Aidan turned back to the conversation he'd been dreading. "Zeb?" he hissed into the phone. "Tell me everything's fine and my part's over. Tell me you'll contact him this morning."

"Contact who?"

"For God's sake! Dominic—H-G that is—is trying to get in touch with me. *You.* Whatever." How did Dominic have Aidan's number? They hadn't exchanged contact details during the date. "You need to sort things out with his PA. Tanya, her name is."

"I know." Zeb's voice was unusually submissive.

"How come someone's calling my phone anyway?"

"I told them I had trouble with mine, so yours was an emergency number."

"You haven't got any trouble with your phone. Have you?"

"Well, no." Zeb sounded evasive. "But I can't take calls at the moment. They probably tried me but couldn't get an answer on my number, so they called yours."

Can't take calls?

"Why can't they just call Lukas at the agency? He arranged all this for you, didn't he? He can sort it out."

Lukas Stefanowicz was Zeb's agent and mentor to both of them. He'd been a significant influence in their lives since their parents died. Fifteen years older than the twins, he was a friend of their mother's and running a talent agency at the time. When Zeb dropped out of college to model, Aidan had asked Lukas to act for Zeb: to manage his blooming career and give him some stability. They both trusted Lukas implicitly.

"They wouldn't have got through to Lukas either. And they wouldn't have got any sense from that idiot twink who runs his desk when he's away."

"When he's…? I didn't know he was away."

"Well, that's the thing, Ade." Now the evasiveness sounded even more strained. "That's what it's all about. I didn't think you needed all the details. You worry too much as it is. Everything was going to be sorted out quickly and quietly, and things would be back to normal before anyone knew."

"What *what* is all about? This is making my head hurt, Zeb. Bad enough I messed it all up last night."

"I'm sure you didn't. You're a bright kid. I should know, right?"

Aidan smiled despite his confusion. His twin's teasing was a familiar comfort. "It was going okay, but then we were ambushed by photographers and I panicked. I fled from the club like a scared rabbit, and I pushed Dominic off like Cinderella seeing midnight approaching at full speed."

"You pushed him off?" Zeb sounded startled. "You mean he was all over you in the first place? And you let him?"

"It wasn't like that."

Zeb gave an unusually brittle laugh. "It's okay, bro. It was all part of the scene. Like I said originally, you didn't have to put out, but it's fine if you want to pretend to have fun—"

"Stop it!" Aidan was surprised at the force of his protest. "Don't try and make it sound like I—like I was playing a game."

"You weren't?"

Dominic's mouth on mine, his hot breath on my neck, his strong hands stroking my thighs—"You know what I mean. The whole evening was a favor to you."

Zeb's voice grew softer. "What really happened between you and H-G?"

"Nothing. Why are you harassing me about it?" The misery made Aidan snappier than usual. "I just followed the script. You and Lukas set all this up, remember? I was to go out on a date, be seen with him, be all cozy with him."

"Not like that, exactly."

"What, then?" Why was Zeb acting in this weird way? Apparently Zeb went out on arranged dates all the time, just for the publicity. He had no scruples where this was concerned. It was Aidan who acted like the blushing virgin, scurrying back under his stone when the spotlight caught him. "Oh forget it. It doesn't matter. I couldn't go through with it any longer, anyway. I'm bloody useless."

"Ade." Zeb's voice was warm now with love and concern. "Of course you're not. I'm sorry, this is all my fault."

"Yes, it bloody well is."

"Okay." Zeb laughed, but it seemed halfhearted. "Was he a bully?"

"Dominic?" Aidan remembered the twinkle in Dominic's eyes and hands that were confident rather than pushy. "Nothing like that. I accused him of trying to seduce me, I think."

"In the middle of a club? Not that I haven't tried it myself a few times."

Aidan had to smile. Zeb's frankness was refreshing and could almost always cheer him up. "I just embarrassed myself."

Zeb's breath hitched. "Wait just a moment. Did you *want* him to seduce you, Ade?"

"Don't be stupid." But Aidan recalled too vividly the excitement that had flowed through him as he perched almost on Dominic's lap, with the lights dim and alcohol warm in his belly, kissing as if there was nothing more glorious to do until the lights went out on the planet itself. "But at least it's all over now."

"Well… back to that." Zeb instantly sobered, Aidan could hear it in his voice. "The thing is, bro, I need you to keep on with the act."

Chapter Fourteen

"WHAT?" Aidan didn't know if the lurch in his chest was due to horror or—surely not—a weird kind of joy.

"Please. You have to. For just a bit longer."

"Zeb, there's no point discussing this anyway. Dominic Hartington-George won't want to work with *me* again."

"Um, but he does. His PA's already been in contact with the agency. The idiot twink managed to take a coherent message from them. They want to make more plans, arrange another date with me. Well, with *you*."

"No way!" What was going on? Aidan wondered if this was what real panic attacks felt like: as if he'd been launched out into space without enough air. "You *have* to take over now."

"Can't."

"*Can't?*" Even to him, it sounded like a squawk.

"I would if I could, Ade, honest. But I can't get back there at the moment."

"Back where?"

"Home. To your place. To Lukas's studio. Any of the above. You have to cover for me."

Aidan bit his lip. *But I can't!* He let the silence run for several beats too long for any person's comfort.

"Ade? Listen." Zeb sounded very tense.

"I am listening." *But I'm not agreeing.* How many times over the years had he agreed to anything Zeb asked, with or without explanation? Yet today, Aidan refused to buckle under. "Where are you, then?"

Another silence.

"What's up, Zeb? You said there was something going on, that you hadn't given me all the details. Are you in trouble?"

This time Zeb's sigh was pained. "I'm fine."

"No, you're not."

"Yeah. I mean, no, I'm not. Pointless trying to fool you, isn't it?"

Aidan smiled a little sadly, even though Zeb couldn't see him. "You're the one who said I was a bright kid." He wished suddenly—fiercely—that Zeb were there with him. They never had any trouble communicating when they were in sight of each other. And then realization hit him. "You're away, you said. And so is Lukas? Tell me everything, Zeb."

A sudden clatter in the kitchen and the smell of cooking bacon reminded Aidan that Titus was still in the flat. And the text message from Dominic was still on the screen, still unanswered. All of that had to be sorted out somehow, but for the moment, the priority was Zeb. And Lukas Stefanowicz too.

Lukas had been such a good friend and support to the twins. He was still a fit man in his early forties, but he'd suffered a mild stroke a few years ago and been told to take things easier at work. At the time, Zeb and Aidan had exchanged cynical looks; Lukas was wedded to his agency, thrived on stress, and was a notorious control freak. But the twins had later agreed that Zeb would keep an eye on Lukas's well-being, whether Lukas liked it or not, and that Aidan would also help out if necessary.

"Is he okay? Oh Zeb, has he—?"

"God, no! He's okay—he's fine. Well, stressed as always, but that's his default, as we both know."

"Have you had a row? I know you don't always get on at work."

"No, no trouble there either. And he's not unreasonable, Ade. He just pushes me to make sure I do my best."

"Right." Aidan didn't remember Zeb's stories in quite the same way, as Zeb had often called late at night ranting about the long hours and physical effort involved in working with Lukas and his crippling deadlines.

"The fact is he had a mild angina attack last month. He's currently booked into a Swiss clinic for a couple of days' rest and to get it all checked out."

"He never said!"

"He didn't want anyone to know, Ade. He still doesn't."

Aidan could see why. Lukas was a prominent, dynamic name on the fashion scene, and Aidan knew what a cutthroat business fashion could be. Lukas wouldn't want his clients to know he was anything less than fully in control of the agency and its schedule.

"But what's that got to do with *you*?" Realization hit again. "Bloody hell!" He must be more tired than he imagined not to connect with Zeb quicker than this.

"Ade? Don't rush to conclusions now—"

"You're with him, aren't you? In Switzerland."

Zeb sighed again, but it was a sappy sound rather than one of frustration.

As if he's blushing?

Aidan could barely remember how a blush looked on Zeb's high, sharp cheekbones, and he hadn't seen him embarrassed since their schooldays. "How long have you two had something going on?" Aidan felt a little hurt that Zeb hadn't confided in him before now.

"It's not going on at all." Zeb sounded miserable. "Well, not like I want. I realized months ago how I felt. There was one night when we were late in the office together, and *Jesus*, he looked so good with his necktie loosened, leaning over my shoulder to look at some designer or other's next season collection and smelling of that Italian cologne and good, old-fashioned sweat, and—oh fuck. Wish I could talk properly to you, bro. Wish we were there together, right?"

"Right," Aidan said softly.

"I tried to broach the subject—to make him see we'd be good together. But Lukas always goes on about being in place of a parent for us, when the last fucking way I think of him is like a dad. We *had* parents, didn't we, Ade? Real ones. That's enough for me. Lukas has come to mean… well, much more than a substitute."

"Oh, Zeb." The pain in his twin's voice was as clear to Aidan as if Zeb really was sitting next to him.

"Fuck. Sorry, bro. Anyway, I had to forget it all when he had the attack. He booked the clinic on his own, like he was trying to keep it from me, dammit, and when I found out, I had to bully him to take me with him, and…. Well, that's how it all went. We were hoping to be back within a few days, and then I'd talk everything through with you." Zeb cleared his throat. "He needs me with him, Ade, whether he'll admit it or not."

"Of course. But why did you ever accept the job with Dominic in the first place? Lukas could have put someone else on it."

"I *wish*. But they asked for me specifically. If I'd refused to do it, they'd have contacted the agency to renegotiate and found Lukas unavailable. He's *never* unavailable, is he? All hell would break loose if the press got hold of that nugget. So if I kept the date, or you did, we had a few days' breathing space to get this trip over with, without anyone suspecting where Lukas is or why."

It sounded convoluted to Aidan's mind, but he supposed Lukas knew what he was doing. But what turmoil in Zeb's life! Aidan wondered how serious Zeb was about Lukas. He'd never heard such emotion in his twin's voice before, not about a man. And how did Lukas feel about Zeb? He'd always been a trusted friend to them both and was happily involved in their lives, especially Zeb's. Aidan had always been content to stay in the background, recognizing the special relationship Lukas and Zeb had. But was that enough to build a romance?

"Ade? I'm sorry." Zeb's voice was truly anguished. "I'm sure it'll just be one more date. Then I'll be back."

"It's okay. Don't rush, for Lukas's sake. It's just…." Aidan couldn't seem to articulate the churning feeling in the pit of his stomach at the thought of continuing the pretense. Was it the lying that disturbed him? The feeling that he was cheating Dominic and his team, offering the man false company and something much less than he wanted? But on the other hand stood his loyalty to Zeb. "I'll handle it. I'll make it work."

He closed the call after a promise from Zeb to let him know how Lukas's checkup was going, then took a long, deep breath.

They want to make more plans, arrange another date with me.

Why the hell would they? The weird thing was that he felt excited rather than horrified. Why did he feel a thrill of anticipation at the thought of seeing Dominic again, even after their last disastrous meeting? Why had Aidan's tangled, champagne-addled dreams been full of a beefy, bearded man with a firm but comforting grip and lips that tasted of red wine and lust?

Good God. I really do need to get out more.

But every time that thought occurred to him, Aidan had visions of striding across the hills with Dominic beside him, both of them pink-cheeked and breathing deeply—and laughing.

He picked up his phone and before he could lose his nerve, called up the number from Dominic's text. It went straight to generic voice mail.

"You have sparkly gel stuff in your hair, kid." Titus boomed in his ear, startling him out of his hazy, rather sensual thoughts. "Have you been out at some kind of a disco?" He thumped a dish of fragrantly steaming bacon and eggs in front of Aidan, with a side plate of hot buttered toast.

Aidan didn't bother informing Titus that no one went to *discos* any longer, and he didn't have time to be his most polite. However, he couldn't ignore his stomach, which grumbled at the sight of the food. "Have you eaten too?"

Titus smirked and raised a mug of tea to Aidan as if in a toast. "Of course, Shakespeare. Oh, and you're out of bacon now. Eggs too. And I know what a healthy appetite you have."

Titus was incorrigible. He was eyeing up Aidan's plate, obviously still hungry. "Eat this with me," Aidan said, "but then you'll have to go. I've got things to do."

He had to get changed into some of Zeb's clothes and get back into role. Then he'd go round to the offices of Dominic's PA—Tanya had given him a business card, if he could peel it out of the back pocket of those painfully tight jeans—and try to find Dominic. That would be so much easier than trying to apologize by phone.

"Acting business?" Titus asked through a mouthful of tea and toast.

"Sort of. I have to go and put something right."

The minute Aidan said it, he knew he wanted that more than anything. And not just for Zeb's sake.

Chapter Fifteen

BY late morning, Dom still didn't want to talk about
the night before, despite his phone ringing off the
hook with calls from reporters. In fact, he unplugged
the bloody thing in the end. He'd sent a groveling
text to Zeb from his phone to the emergency number
Zeb's agency had given him—well, it was meant to be
groveling, but perhaps Dom wasn't the most efficient
texter on the planet—and then turned that off as well.

Dom just wasn't cut out for all this angst and panic.
Mountains were so much easier to deal with than men.
They didn't answer back, or express shock, or look so
sexy in ridiculous clothes, or taste so damn delicious….

"Just take it easy," Tanya had said. But that wasn't
Dom's way, was it? He wasn't used to this world of
social chatter and charm. Dominic Hartington-George

told things exactly as he saw them. And that was usually far too blunt for his audience.

He felt really bad about the evening with Zeb Z. He'd been prepared to write the whole thing off as a really bad idea when Zeb shot out of the club like a gazelle sighting a shotgun, but Tanya was forcing him to face up to it and rethink. Had Zeb's flight been a lucky escape for Dom—or a surprisingly bitter disappointment?

Where did it all go wrong?

Zeb had been… not what Dom had expected. He'd anticipated a flippant, flighty thing with a head full of nothing but fashion. But Dom had spent a large chunk of time today reading more online interviews with famous models, and it was becoming clear to him that they worked bloody hard, came from all backgrounds, and had as much good or bad to say as any other damn person he met in life.

And Zeb had been a glowing example of a young man Dom would have been pleased to spend more time with if he, Dom, hadn't been so buoyed up with prejudice and resentment. The guy talked about climbing and listened to Dom's stories and opinions with genuine sense and interest. His stories of the modeling world had been amusing, almost as if he'd been a fellow spectator like Dom rather than involved in it so intimately himself. He was articulate and intelligent, and wasn't so up his own arse that he didn't tease Dom when it was deserved.

Yes, Dom could be a blunt bastard, but he also knew when he was being an arse and when he needed taking down a peg or two.

And then… the touching thing, at the club: "It's natural we'll touch and be close." Right. But that had been the first step down the slippery slope. The minute Dom slid his hand around Zeb's shoulders, he'd felt a rather odd but delicious warmth steal through him.

Like it was a *real* date.

What a poor, sorry sap he was!

Tanya's right, I need to get out more.

The first touch of a fit young man and he'd melted inside. *Bizarre.* And then instead of treating the guy with respect and care, he'd pawed all over him. Had it been because of the drink? It had loosened both their tongues. First the chatting and the joking…. And, oh my God! The *hairy thing.* He groaned aloud at the memory of his clumsy joking about bears. What the hell had he been playing at?

He wandered into his kitchen, opened the fridge, shut it again. Turned on the kettle, switched it off. Food and drink didn't tempt or soothe him as they usually would. He was restless because he had to sort things out. Dom didn't shirk his duty, however unpleasant, and he always got things done. Those skills made him an excellent leader on a climb but didn't seem to translate into normal, London-based life. His mother always relished pointing that out to him. Only the last time she'd visited, she'd scorned his frustration at not having the money to mount the Eiger expedition.

"I can't help that," she'd said crisply. "Your father and his ancestors have never had a head for money. If I hadn't invested what money I brought to the family in property, we'd be living on the charity of others by now."

Dom had almost bitten his tongue in half, trying not to point out that his high-handed mother hadn't engendered any charitable feelings in anyone he'd ever met. "I'm not asking for charity. When my book comes out, I'll be able to repay a lot of the debts."

Or so his publisher had told him. They'd been thrilled with the photos from previous expeditions, but he had to finish the current climbing program before they'd consider a release slot.

"Well, don't come to me," she'd said. "I barely have enough to maintain a decent social calendar in town. Can't you find some rich man to support your wandering ways?" She managed to make it sound as if he were philandering rather than mountaineering. His parents might have accepted him being gay, but they still had some pretty deeply ingrained prejudices about the "lifestyle."

"It doesn't work like that," he snapped. "At least, not for me."

His mother's look had been odd. "Do you mean to tell me you're a romantic at heart, just like your father?"

Dom had been startled. Somehow he'd never considered his imposing, adventurous father as a hearts-and-flowers man.

"Oh, not toward me." At seeing the look on his face, she'd sighed rather bitterly. "The romance was all for his beloved mountains."

"I'm not like that," Dom had protested.

He had more to offer, didn't he? He could offer a man something other than holding the fort back at home while he, Dom, traveled the world and conquered the elements. If he found a man he wanted to make those sacrifices for, of course.

Unbidden, Zeb's face popped into his mind. And when he refocused on where he was and what he was doing, he found he was holding a dishcloth in his right hand and—inexplicably—a single egg in the other. His mind was so far off-kilter he was scaring himself.

Well, there was only one thing for it. He had to make this right, and not just for the sponsors either. He glanced around but couldn't see where he'd slung his phone. He ought to see if Zeb had replied to his text— if he'd even acknowledged him. But maybe he'd go around to Zeb's agency first and see if he could find the model there. That had to be better than a bald message.

Yes, that was a decent plan.

He grabbed his jacket and flung open his front door, where a blizzard of flashbulbs assaulted him.

"Dom!"

"Dom, are you going to meet Zeb Z?"

The photographers hung over his front hedge, regardless of any potential damage to the foliage or their clothes. Dom made a mental note to ask the young man who did his garden maintenance whether they could embed barbed wire in the shrubbery. Reporters called eagerly from behind the cameras, as if Dom would be remotely interested in engaging with them. He would rather have torn off his left arm and fed it to a passing dog. Or perhaps a reporter's arm would be more rewarding, for both the dog and Dom.

"Dom! Over here, let's have a shot!"

"How long have you two been dating? What do you talk about?"

"Is he in charge of your wardrobe now?"

"Dom, how about a word for our readers?"

Dom drew a deep, *deep* breath. He wouldn't normally censor the actual word he was tempted to give "our readers," but Tanya's words about taking it easy rang clearly in his memory. He suddenly imagined Zeb's face after reading the headlines in the gossip press if Dom actually spewed the profanities he was currently thinking.

A feeling even more bizarre.... Dom couldn't ever remember worrying what a man thought of him before doing exactly what he bloody well wanted.

He struggled through the crowd toward his SUV, with his lips pursed shut and sporting the most intimidating frown he could manage. He slammed the door temptingly near a reporter's hand and revved the engine until they all scattered out of his way.

"Is he in charge of your wardrobe now?"

Bloody hell.

Chapter Sixteen

AIDAN leapt the stairs to the exit at Holborn station two at a time, keen to get to the street and make his way to Long Acre, where Tanya's office was. More than a few people stared curiously at him, but he relied on their British reserve to keep them at a distance, and people's natural disbelief that they'd actually see someone famous struggling on the daytime Tube. Plus the whole Covent Garden area of London was a media center. It was nothing unusual to see celebrities there—in fact, Lukas's agency was just around the corner on Macklin Street. But if he hadn't wanted to draw attention, maybe he shouldn't have used so much of Zeb's products—Aidan's hair seemed to spike up in a completely different way from his twin's—or maybe the padded jacket with its Union Jack fur collar and diamanté-studded seams had been overkill.

Good grief, this model lifestyle is fraught with pitfalls.

In a hurry, he rounded a corner by one of the small Italian cafés and ran straight into another man. The familiarity of the cologne hit him a millisecond before he recognized the build of—

"Dominic!"

"Zeb!" The other man leaned back, just as shocked. They stared at each other for a full twenty seconds.

"I'm on my way to find you—" Aidan finally started.

"—On my way to apologize—" Dominic broke in.

They both stopped talking, then tried again—but at the same time—and stopped again. Dom started to laugh, and loudly. A clutch of businessmen in smart suits swerved around them in alarm, and a hiss of brakes from a passing bus made them dodge back into the shelter of the café.

Finally, Dom calmed down enough to ask, "Will you join me for a coffee?"

Aidan, smiling in return, looked at him more carefully. He'd forgotten what a twinkle there was in Dominic's eyes, what passion and strength of character they hinted at. "Yes, that'd be good. Is here okay?"

"Of course," Dominic said, though he didn't take his gaze off Aidan's face and as far as Aidan could see, hadn't even glanced into the café. But Dominic's tone was one of obvious relief.

They did the you-first dance in the doorway until Dominic gave a snort of frustration and pushed Aidan inside ahead of him. Aidan wandered over to a free table toward the back of the room, sat down, and picked up the brightly colored laminated menu.

"I've ordered us both latte and carrot cake," Dominic said abruptly, appearing at the seat beside him.

Aidan blinked hard, then caught sight of the sumptuously thick cake under a clear dome on the counter and nodded happy agreement.

Dominic's face twisted with a strange kind of grimace. "I mean. If that's all right with you."

"Yes, it's great. I love carrot cake."

Dominic sat down but seemed very restless.

Aidan peered at him. "Are you okay? Do you want to go somewhere else?"

"God, no. Or maybe… if you do?"

Aidan laughed. "What's going on? Why are you being so weird?"

"Weird?"

"Dominic, you know what I mean. You're being… oh, I don't know. Considerate, maybe? *Nice*?"

Dominic looked as horrified at the description as if he'd been smacked in the face with a frying pan.

"Exactly," Aidan said, dryly. "I may not have known you for long, but you're not acting your usual assertive self."

Their coffees arrived and Dominic didn't answer immediately, but he was clearly impatient for the waitress to move away again. Aidan made sure he smiled extra gratefully at her, and even asked if she could bring over another pot of sugar sachets. They sat for another couple of minutes in silence until she brought over the sugar and then bustled away again.

"Are you bloody teasing me?" Dominic hissed.

"Yes," Aidan replied quite calmly. And then grinned. "I can't resist. It's a bit of a coup, I imagine, to have Dominic Hartington-George worrying about my wants and needs."

"You make me sound a right selfish tosser."

"No," Aidan said softly, dropping his gaze to his milky coffee. "But you can make yourself sound like that. I wish you'd take better care, for your own sake." When he looked up again, Dominic was staring at him. "You said, in your message, you wanted to talk."

"I realized straightaway I'd behaved badly," Dominic said in a gruff rush. "Last night. What kind of a bully was I?"

"No, you weren't." Aidan couldn't bear that confused, anguished look on Dominic's face, and hurried to reassure him. "How stupid was I, for that matter? Panicking at the sight of a few cameras when we were in a public bar and should have been expecting it."

"We were planning on it. At least, according to our publicists."

"Yes. We were." Aidan felt a wisp of strange sadness. "That's not the real issue, though, is it?"

Dominic's eyes looked very fierce over the rim of his coffee cup. Aidan could see the waitress taking the long way across the room so that she didn't come too close to their table again. "What do you mean?"

"If you're anything like me, you're not shy or apologetic about the attention. But why should you have to put up with it when you're on a night out, or when you don't want to be disturbed, or when you're…?"

Aidan waited for Dominic to finish the sentence, but he didn't. "Kissing?" Aidan ventured, astounded at his own boldness. He met Dominic's startled gaze with his own. For a long moment, they fell silent again. *Remembering?* Aidan felt a slow blush start to creep up his neck. He stabbed his fork into his cake and took a huge bite.

Dominic tilted his head, his expression quizzical. "You're a mischievous kind of fellow, Zeb. Sharp. And witty too."

"You mean, for a model?"

"And still full of issues, I see," Dominic said wryly.

Aidan laughed and some cake crumbs sprayed back out onto his plate. The café was full of the warm aroma of brewing coffee and rich pastry. He was ridiculously happy at seeing Dominic again. Who cared if he was being rash? "You're right. Who am I to nose away at your business when we're just here for promotional purposes?"

Dominic winced very slightly. "Yes. Of course we are. But I like it."

"I'm… sorry? You like what?"

Dominic paused before replying. He reached a hand to Aidan's face and brushed off a cake crumb that still clung to his cheek. "I like your nosiness. Your wit. Your sharpness."

Aidan gave up trying to rationalize what was happening and stuck out his hand. "Let's shake on a joint apology, right?"

When Dominic shook enthusiastically, Aidan bit back a grimace from its firmness.

"And how about another chance?" Dominic said gruffly.

"Sorry?" Aidan kept repeating apologies all the time. He couldn't imagine Zeb doing that.

"Will you go on another date?" Dominic picked up his coffee cup, then put it down again too sharply. He flushed. "Dammit. I mean, please?" Aidan shook his head and laughed. "What the hell—?"

"No, I'm sorry." At Dominic's bemused expression, he continued. "I'm not laughing at you. I just didn't expect… I was just surprised. At you wanting to go out again. I thought I was too uptight for you."

"You were too…? *You?*"

Aidan felt the blush rising right up to his cheeks. He and Dominic were a pair of precious, easily embarrassed blossoms. "I was on my way to ask the same thing of you. A second date, that is."

"You were? Well, that makes it all perfectly right again. Doesn't it? Unless that shake of your head means you've changed your mind?"

"No. I mean, yes. It was just surprise." *Just pleasure.* Aidan couldn't stop smiling. "Things do seem to be okay again. Though I'm mortified at the stupid things I said, about you treating me like a mountain peak to climb."

Dominic waved his hand dismissively. "What about my growling like a real bear, trying to tempt you with my chest hair, for God's sake?"

They laughed together. Dominic didn't seem to be able to drag his eyes away from Aidan's mouth, while Aidan wondered if it was too soon to ask for the second date right now. Then something caught his eye over Dominic's shoulder. "Isn't that your PA's assistant outside the café?"

"Eric? Where?" Dominic swiveled around in his chair.

Eric was clearly peering in through the café window at them. He had a cardboard holder with four coffees in one hand and was waving at Dom with the other. "Hello!" he called, though they could barely hear it from inside. He looked very excited. "Dom! I'm over here!"

Dominic gave a groan. "I refused to go into the office today, but I never imagined he'd be roaming the bloody streets stalking me."

"That's paranoia talking," Aidan scoffed. "He's probably just on a coffee run." More movement from behind Eric distracted him again. People were clustering up against the front window. There was the flash of a camera. "Oh, for God's sake."

"What?"

"More reporters." Aidan's heart sank. "They must be following one or other of us."

"Or Eric's on their payroll," Dominic grumbled. "But we'll show them. Now's the time to start afresh, isn't it?" He quickly swallowed his last mouthful of cake, pushed his chair back, and stood. He held his hand out to Aidan.

Aidan let himself be pulled upright. Dominic's hand was large and strong. "You mean… the publicity thing?"

Dominic's expression faltered but only for the merest of seconds. "Of course. That's what I meant."

Dominic threw down some money before Aidan could offer to pay his share for the coffee—and it looked way too much, even with the generous tip the waitress deserved—but he decided not to mention it. Dominic had the look of a man on a mission. The other café patrons watched in alarm as the two men weaved quickly through the tables and made a dash for the door. Cameras flashed again and people called out to them. The café owner on duty behind the counter just rolled his eyes as if he was used to this media nonsense all the time.

"My car's parked by Tanya's office," Dominic muttered to Aidan out of the corner of his mouth. "Will you come back to my place? Then we can—"

"—plan strategy?" Aidan gasped back. "I hear you."

But it was a struggle to get through the small crowd outside the shop, made more awkward by the lunchtime office workers and sundry tourists now filling the pavements, intrigued by the unfolding drama. Dominic and Aidan pushed forward, making their way toward Long Acre, but the reporters followed a few steps behind.

One particularly strident man kept yelling over the others until his voice was the only one Aidan could hear. "Dom! Zeb!"

Dominic gave a grumble that sounded like "fuck off" and maneuvered Aidan in front of him, shielding him from the followers.

"The model and the mountaineer! London's answer to *Brokeback Mountain*! Who plays base camp?"

At that last comment, Dominic stopped abruptly, spun back around, and located the obnoxious reporter. He was only a foot away and skidded to a halt before he could crash into Dominic's heels.

"Dominic?" Aidan was horribly worried he knew what was coming next. "Wait!"

Dominic ignored him. He took one step forward, swung his fist with confident ease, and punched the reporter on the nose.

Chapter Seventeen

DOM made the sprint to the underground car park where
he'd parked his car without any problem, grateful every
second of the way that he'd kept up with his training at
the local gym. Zeb had less stamina, though, despite Dom
dragging him along behind him. He was still gasping five
minutes later as he leaned against Dom's SUV, regaining
his breath. Dom guessed the fashion types didn't get much
genuine exercise when they worked in town. Or maybe
it was some kind of shock? Zeb's eyes still looked rather
large and his skin was paler than usual. Mind you, Dom
reckoned he'd look a lot healthier if he washed out those
stupid glitter gel highlights and let the rich chestnut-
brown roots grow out.

   Dom shook his hand surreptitiously down by his
side. The knuckles smarted. He hadn't punched anyone

in a long time, but it had been the perfect distraction, letting them escape the rabble. There was no sound or sight of the reporters, so it looked like they'd shaken them off. But for how long? He wondered, only slightly guiltily, if he should pop into Tanya's office across the street and explain his position before her phone started ringing with complaints. But hell, that was what he employed a PA for, wasn't it?

Zeb's cry startled him. "What the hell did you do that for? Punching someone—it's outrageous!"

Dominic set his jaw into a familiar, mulish state. "Didn't you hear what he said?"

"Well, yes, but what does that matter? Zeb's used to stupid abuse."

Dominic frowned. "Why do you talk about yourself in the third person?"

"What?" Zeb's eyes widened even farther. "I mean, we have to get out of here. What if he calls the police? What if he sues you?"

"I don't care," Dominic said. "And maybe we should stand our ground."

There was a sudden clatter of footsteps and Dom tensed. But the man who came down the ramp into the car park was Eric. His eyes shining with mischief, he crowed, "Bloody well done, Dom! That rat bastard's caused all sorts of problems for other clients of Tanya's. Time he got his comeuppance!"

Dominic braced himself in case the horde was right behind Eric, baying for blood. "Just let me at him again—"

"No! Let's get going," Zeb pleaded beside him.

Eric nodded emphatically. "Zeb's right. You should keep a low profile right now. Tanya will smooth it over, and we'll sort out a proper media schedule now we know you two are back together."

"Wait—" Zeb's protest was weak.

"I've got it covered!" Eric announced gleefully. "You two can just go!" And with a final thumbs-up to Dom, he turned and ran back up the ramp, out of sight.

Dom shook the car keys out of his pocket and made his way to the driver's side. "Hop in. I know the best way across the city in less than half an hour."

Zeb didn't move, but he took a long, deep breath. "There's just one thing to get straight before we go." His voice was tight. "You didn't need to thump that reporter on my behalf. Despite my stupid behavior the other night, I'm not some shrinking virgin. All gay men suffer abuse at some stage. And I'm a gay man."

Dom took a breath before speaking too. Had he made another mistake? There were too many bloody sinkholes in the dating path for his liking. He came back around the vehicle to stand a respectful distance from Zeb. "You're a *man*, Zeb. Yes, a man who happens to be gay, but everyone has the equal right to respect."

Zeb stared back at him.

Is that amusement in his eyes?

"Dominic, you have no idea how sweepingly fabulous that statement is. Is that how you treat everyone? As complete equals?"

Dom nodded, puzzled. "Of course. At least until they prove themselves to be complete morons."

Zeb laughed. He looked more relaxed now, and his eyes glittered in the fluorescent lights of the car park. "You don't suffer fools gladly, do you?"

"No, I don't. But not everyone's a fool."

"No?"

"No," Dom said more slowly. "Like you, for example." Dom had the feeling something was shifting between them; maybe it already had. His earlier apology had been necessary, no question of it. Now Zeb's body language implied he was as eager to be near Dom as he had been last night, but this time Zeb's expression was one of genuine, light-of-day, sober understanding. Dom was fascinated by how Zeb's eyes looked with the pupils dilated, and how Zeb's mouth hitched up at the side when he smiled… and how elegantly he leaned against the car, his delicate but very masculine fingers pressed against the passenger window.

Dom couldn't help himself—which was a surprise to him—and he leaned in to Zeb. To his delight, Zeb caught his shoulder, drawing him closer. Dom cupped Zeb's face in his hands and, just for a second, breathed on Zeb's lips.

Good God. The mere temptation was enough to make Dom's cock harden.

"What are you waiting for?" Zeb asked softly. "You weren't nervous in the club last night."

"That's exactly why I'm bloody waiting," Dom said. "It's your call."

Zeb laughed. It was a high, melodic sound, like a man who spoke for his living, not one who posed like a voiceless mannequin. Dom was almost painfully aware of Zeb's body, but it was the man's character that shone from his eyes at this very moment, fascinating and seducing Dom in equal measure.

Zeb's eyelids fluttered half closed. "My call is… yes please."

Dom gave a strangled grunt—he wasn't able to articulate anything more eloquent—and pressed his mouth on Zeb's.

Oh, but it was good! The kiss last night in the club had been hot and needy, but this time Zeb's mouth was cooler and softer. Dom slid his hand around Zeb's waist, and they clung together for blissful minutes, tasting each other. Dom remembered feeling like this as a teenager, when he first discovered boys were so bloody exciting and sexy. Kissing felt new all over again! His cock hardened further inside his jeans, and the skin between his shoulder blades shivered with goose bumps. His palms itched to touch Zeb, to hold him tightly, to put his mouth to Zeb's shoulder, chest, hip… to bring skin to skin. To stretch out beside him, naked, glorious, free to touch and laugh and fuck, and to share that with someone who felt the same. Yet for the moment, all he wanted to do was run his tongue gently around Zeb's mouth and caress his lips. He could taste the remnants of carrot cake, smell a sharp grapefruit cologne that he'd come to associate with Zeb, and hear Zeb's soft pants of pleasure against his cheek. Zeb's arms were slim but muscled, and his hips were narrow but solid where they pressed against Dom's.

Too much clothing—yet Dom was almost desperate to hold on to the wonderful creature. Through the heady swim of desire in his head, he realized that he didn't want Zeb to slip away from him again.

It was a long time before he broke away from the kissing.

Zeb gazed up at Dom. His hair looked tousled and his eyes were even brighter than before. He whispered, "I think you should drop me at the Tube station."

Dom struggled to calm his breathing. "I don't want to."

Zeb laughed raggedly. "I don't think I want you to either. But I also don't think…. Well, I want to mull all this over calmly, in my own time."

Dom was awash with disappointment, but what could he do? He'd crowded the guy last time and that had ended horribly. Now they'd made up, things were back on an even keel—and he was in danger of sabotaging it again. He took a slow step backward. "I can take you home."

"No." Zeb looked away for a brief moment as if confused. "I'd prefer the Tube. I… I'd like to make my own way."

"But maybe…?" Dom cleared his throat. "Maybe you'll come back to mine for a drink another time? A rain check, as Eric says. Just a drink. No pressure. No strings."

Zeb stared at him for so long that Dom thought he'd messed things up again. He wondered if a takeaway carrot cake would work reconciliation a second time. Maybe the challenge would require double-chocolate muffins and one of those Bakewell tarts as well….

"Yes." Zeb's cheeks were a very fetching pink. "I'd like that."

Chapter Eighteen

A COUPLE of Fridays later, Aidan made the trip to Holborn Tube station again, but this time with a much lighter step—and a less glamorous look.

It had been another week of living his odd brand of double life. He'd put all his directing on hold, with an excuse to the Dreamweavers that he was brainstorming new ideas. He stayed in his flat working on scripts most of the time, contacting friends only by phone and e-mail, and ordering his groceries for home delivery.

At least Zeb had come through with some of the "date fee," as Aidan named it, so Aidan's financial crisis was temporarily over. But he was terrified of being spotted as Zeb if he went out and about... and then terrified he'd be spotted as *Not Zeb*. The whole thing was getting tortuous.

The one good thing about it all had been more dates with Dominic. Nothing too extravagant—just a couple of far more entertaining movies, a visit to a new Outward Bound center, and a fashion chain store opening. It meant they were "seen" in public as dating, but it was on a far less frenetic level. Apparently there'd been a major scandal on *Celebrity Big Brother*, and for a while at least, no one was interested in other celebrity stories. The reporter with the bloody nose seemed to have dropped off the scene—thankfully without suing Dominic, as far as Aidan knew—and they were in a hiatus period with the media. He and Dominic allowed a few snaps and quotes when they were out and about in London, in return for the end of harassment. It was a kind of truce.

They made a very striking couple, according to Tanya. Dominic had a habit of slipping his arm around Aidan's waist in public and nuzzling into his neck. And Aidan couldn't help but arch up against him when he did. It was a Pavlovian response, wasn't it? Not his fault at all. But there'd been quite a few pictures of them in that pose in the newspapers.

Whatever the public response, the dates had become the highlights in Aidan's life. After his initial caution, he readily agreed to follow the next date with drinks back at Dominic's house. They'd watched an adventure movie, which had enough charm to keep Aidan amused as well as Dom—though maybe it was the company that charmed Aidan? They'd drunk another bottle of good wine and eaten late-night scrambled eggs and bacon, even though Aidan protested Dominic used too many eggs. Dominic had just quoted James Bond's creator Ian Fleming, who'd apparently included a recipe in one book calling for twelve eggs. Urban myth

claimed he said "Anything else just dirties the pan."
It had made Aidan laugh, as so much of Dominic's
outrageous behavior did, to the extent he suspected
Dominic played it up just to amuse him. The meal had
been ridiculously tasty, and then he'd taken a cab home.

No pressure. No strings.

There was no mistaking the sexual tension between
them. They touched each other gently and easily: an
arm across the shoulders, a brush of fingers against
the hip. And the kisses were.... Aidan, despite his
command of the English language, was still trying to
find words to describe them. He'd kissed plenty of men
in his time, of course—though only a fraction of Zeb's
tally, if anyone were keeping score—and he could be
as passionate as the next guy. At least, he could be if
he let down his defenses. Every time Dominic kissed
him, Aidan wanted to let them down—and fast. The
hairs on his skin lifted with goose bumps and his cock
started filling. The excitement that shuddered through
him made him feel like a heroine in one of the historical
plays he'd directed early in his drama-school career.
Of course, Aidan was far removed from those virginal
ladies. None of them had had such a responsive dick or
the sudden urge to grab Dominic by the arms and push
him up against the wall, thrust a hand down to cup his
impressive groin, and just *plunder* his damn mouth!

God. Aidan leant briefly against the wall outside
the Tube station and drew a deep breath, trying to calm
his libido. He was due to meet Dominic just around the
corner from Tanya's office, and then they were going to
a photography exhibition at a nearby gallery. It would
be an impromptu visit, though they'd probably attract
attention before long. Aidan was easing himself out of
his Zeb persona, whether consciously or subconsciously,

and he found himself mixing Zeb's wardrobe with his own clothes. He'd stopped touching up his gelled hair, and he didn't bother with more daily makeup than absolutely necessary. Though to be honest, he was pretty fond of the eyeliner by now. Aidan had always enjoyed making up for the stage, and more than once he'd found Dominic staring fascinated at his eyes with a dark, needy gaze....

God, the libido again!

Smiling to himself, he turned into Long Acre, and there was Dominic coming toward him, oblivious to the people who scattered to either side of his determined stride along the pavement. Aidan pulled himself together and waved in welcome.

Dominic paused in front of him, smiling back. "I like the new look."

"The new look?" Had he forgotten something critical to Zeb, to his role?

"Take that panicked look off your face. I mean you seem more relaxed. More normal." When Aidan started to laugh, Dominic scowled. "You seem to find me amusing all the bloody time."

Aidan couldn't mistake the gleam of pleasure in Dominic's eyes, giving the lie to his complaint. "I don't mean it that way, you know I don't. It's a happy feeling, not mockery. It's...." Aidan shrugged, unable to express it well enough. "You make me feel good, that's all I can say. You're a very unique and exciting person."

"Me?" Dominic sounded skeptical, but there was a rosy flush on his cheeks.

He's so bloody handsome. Aidan enjoyed just looking at him. He was also getting to know Dominic's moods and reactions, which was a new and thrilling experience. He hadn't felt this spark with a man for years. Okay, so they'd only known each other for a couple of weeks and this was hardly a normal relationship, yet he trusted Dominic to be frank with him, and he'd relaxed very quickly and easily into Dominic's company. *Oh God*, maybe Dominic didn't feel the same?

But it seemed he did. "I know what you mean," Dominic was saying. "You and I think the same way on the important things. And as for everything else, apparently I appreciate the occasional challenge. I'm sure Tanya would say I need it. What's more, dammit, you make me see some fun in life. You're good for me too. No point in lying about these things, is there?" Dominic turned to lead the way toward the gallery.

And yet it's all based on a lie. The thought hit Aidan with stronger force than ever. "Dominic," he blurted. Dominic paused and turned back, still smiling. "I… there's something… I need to tell you something."

An ambulance was coming up the street, weaving its way around parked cars and bunches of pedestrians. Its siren was deafening this close. A group of teenagers in school uniform passed them, chattering noisily in a foreign language. Dominic tilted his head, concentrating on listening to Aidan. "What is it?" He frowned expectantly.

Aidan opened his mouth again, but nothing would come out. And then, over Dominic's shoulder, he saw them—Titus and Wendy, walking arm in arm down the street, on a direct course toward Aidan and Dominic. *Oh shit!* What were they doing here? *Right* here? Was it just a day out for them, or were they on business? Aidan couldn't remember where their theatrical agent was based. Shit. *Shit!* Wasn't it likely it'd be up here, in the same area of London as Dominic's agent?

Aidan was filled with panic. They'd see him within seconds. Would they recognize him? They had no idea he had a twin, so if he looked enough like Zeb... but maybe he didn't! Or not enough to avoid their curiosity and having them calling out his name—his real name—across the street. And it would be in that booming voice Titus used for the very last row of the Upper Circle; he would shout out for everyone to hear that Aidan Vincent was wearing weird clothes, had his hair full of glitter gel, and who the hell did he think he was pretending to be?

"Quick!" Aidan grabbed Dominic's arm. "Take this route." He pulled Dominic in the opposite direction and dodged into a side road. He kept going, desperate to put distance between them and his Dreamweaver friends before they discovered him.

Several turnings later, Aidan thought it was safe to stop and gather his wits.

"Are you all right?" Dominic looked very confused, although unlike Aidan, he was not at all puffed. "You know this is in the opposite direction to the gallery?"

Aidan suddenly realized where they were: by complete coincidence, a few doors away from the Lukas Stefanowicz Agency—Zeb's base. The last place Aidan wanted to be!

The call from behind him startled him further.

"Zeb? Yes, I was right, it *is* you! Zeb, *sweetie*, over here!"

Aidan remembered at the last minute to turn in response. He didn't want to get used to answering as Zeb—but for the moment, he still *was* Zeb. At this rate he'd be in schizophrenia therapy for the next ten years.

At least it wasn't a reporter this time.

A slight young man hurried down the steps from Lukas's agency and across the road to meet them. He had long blond hair in complicated dreadlocks, the pale, fresh skin of a Scandinavian, and was wearing a vivid neon T-shirt and holey-kneed jeans, plus a broad smile of welcome on his face. "Zeb, thank *God* you're here! I thought you were out on assignment. Lukas has you booked out for another few *weeks*."

Aidan swallowed hard. Was that how long he had to keep this up? He thought of his last evening with Dominic—their talk, their laughter, their touches—and something twisted inside him. He wanted Dominic more and more, but the longer this went on, the more complex the pretense got. Lies had never been digestible to him.

"Just fifteen minutes, right?"

Aidan focused back on the earnest young man in front of him. "Fifteen—? What for?"

The man grinned at him. "*Always* the jokes! That's why they like to work with you. You're professional, but you're such *fun* as well."

"Yes. Sure." Aidan had a low, sick feeling in his gut. "Tell me what's going on."

The guy looked briefly confused, then gabbled on. "*CCC* called. They won't wait until next month. Not one *day*! Could you do a quick session *now*, sweetie? Just to keep them *teased*?" He looked Aidan quickly up and down. "You look fine. Just a little more makeup and perhaps a restyle of the hair. What *have* you been doing with it since I last saw you?" He hurried on without letting Aidan reply. His speech was peppered with virtual italics. "Anyway, I just finished the location shoot with Blake and Elaine, I've been out of the loop for *so* long, but here on my first day back they said, 'Sven, we must have *Zeb*, see if you can find him, today, *right now*!' I mean, I know what a *stickler* Lukas is for his schedule—"

"Yes, and so I don't really have time—"

"—but they *are* one of the top underwear brands, aren't they?"

"They... yes, of course they are," Aidan said weakly. He cast a pleading look at Dominic.

Dominic had been watching the interchange with his usual bemused cynicism. Now he peered at Sven as if he were a new kind of talking bug. "What's the problem?"

There was an awkward moment of silence while Sven and Dominic both gazed at Aidan expectantly. Aidan cleared his throat. "Er... Sven. Remind us both about it, will you?"

Sven shrugged and pushed back some dreads that had fallen forward over his shoulder. "Sure. CCC is a really *big* client. Zeb's due on a shoot for them next month, but they've called the agency and are very *insistent* they want some early mock-ups, like *now*."

"CCC?" Dominic wrinkled his nose.

Aidan closed his eyes. *Hell's bells.* He'd heard Zeb mention them.

"Cup Crotch Company," Sven said merrily. "Only *the* brand for this year's underwear! They *love* Zeb's look, it's *exactly* what they want for the new campaign."

"Cup. Crotch. Company." Dominic repeated each word slowly and deliberately as if waiting for someone from *Candid Camera* to leap out and point a gleeful finger.

Aidan wanted the pavement to open up and swallow him. There was no way he could go inside the

agency on any pretext, least of all in the guise of his
twin. He sneaked a sideways glance at Dominic. "It's a
pity... um, Sven, but I'm booked elsewhere. Anyway,
you'll never get a team together on such short notice—"

"It's all arranged!" Sven's grin got almost
impossibly wider. "Isn't that *lucky*? The studio's been
set up *today* for reviewing the shots from my trip." He
turned briefly to Dominic. "Blake and Elaine—they're
the faces of January Cosmetics, you know?"

"No," Dominic said with his usual bluntness.

"*The Look to Share*," Sven trilled. Aidan reckoned
that if there'd been background music, Sven would
have sung his way through the full commercial. "'The
couple who make up together, *make out* together.' You
get it?"

Dominic opened his mouth but Aidan rushed to
interrupt. "Sven, I can't do it." He gestured toward
Dominic. "I mean, I have a prior engagement."

"Prior eng—?" Sven looked Dominic up and down
with blatant approval. "How *adorable*."

"It's fine with me," Dominic said, in his deep, no-
nonsense voice. His deep, no-nonsense, drop-Aidan-in-
the-shit voice.

"What?" Aidan stared at him. "I can't... I mean,
I'm not in the right mood for modeling right now."
Modeling? And *underwear?*

"We *love* Zeb's moods," Sven said blithely, tilting
his head as if sharing a secret with Dominic. "They add
that extra *edge* to a shoot, you know?"

"I'm sure," Dominic said.

Was that a smirk teasing the edge of his mouth?
Aidan was going to kill him.

Chapter Nineteen

BEFORE Aidan could protest any more, Sven had shooed him across the road and into the agency.

Lukas had converted the top floor into a small private studio, but Aidan had never been there. Luckily he remembered enough from Zeb's tales to know where things were, and he didn't have to hesitate when Sven hustled them up the stairs. Sven flung open the door on the top landing to reveal a spacious and well-lit area with a blank backdrop curtain and standing photographic equipment. The other people in the room turned to stare as Sven, Aidan, and Dominic entered.

"And you'll be working again with your favorite, Zeb, won't you?" Sven crowed.

"I will?" *Dammit, I sound like a parrot.*

"Benjy McAdam, of course! All these years he's been your *favorite* photographer."

"He has?" Aidan said weakly. "I mean, he has." He took a quick peek around the room. Panic rippled through him. Was Benjy the tall man with horn-rimmed spectacles or the plump guy whose T-shirt left a gap above his jeans every time he reached over? After their initial interest, both had turned away to fiddle with the cameras.

Then a tall man approached from the side of the room and drew a startled Aidan into a hug. He wore a T-shirt with a Chinese logo on it and stylish faded jeans, and he'd tied his hair back into a stubby ponytail at his nape. Featureswise he seemed nothing out of the ordinary, but he had a surprisingly confident grip.

"B-Benjy?"

The man pulled back to reveal a face transformed by a mischievous and very attractive smile. "Good to see you too, punk. You're a welcome antidote to that terrible twosome, Flake and Pain."

Dominic snorted a laugh behind them and Sven frowned. "Now, Benjy, you know they're Blake and Elaine. Please don't be so *provocative*." He flipped his hair back again and spoke to Aidan. "Anyway, this is only a few shots, a quick precampaign taster. They tell me it's just a simple 'the making of' video release on YouTube."

"YouTube?" Now Aidan's voice was a squeak.

Sven looked slyly at Dominic. "And you can watch of course, Mr Adorable Engagement."

Aidan glared at Dominic. Yes, that was definitely the start of a smirk… and there was a devilish twinkle in his eyes.

Benjy was cleaning the lens of his camera, but he watched Dominic and Aidan with interest. Aidan thought he caught a brief glimpse of confusion in Benjy's expression when it rested on Aidan. Was Benjy suspicious of "Zeb"?

But before Aidan could say anything else, Sven plumped a hand at the base of his back and propelled him toward a door marked Private. "Hop off and change *there*, sweetie. Half an hour, didn't I say?"

"You said fifteen minutes," Aidan protested.

Sven pressed a bundle of clothing into Aidan's arms and closed the door firmly behind him. Aidan found himself in a small changing closet, clutching a pile of brightly colored, barely decent underwear. What was happening? He couldn't model anything! He had no idea how to, to say nothing of not having the right look—even if he'd been sure what that actually was. Yes, he'd watched Zeb prance about many times at home, practicing, joking, telling entertaining stories about successes and disasters on set. But that was far from doing it himself. Like, a million miles too far!

Then he remembered Zeb's unusually shaky voice and pleading tone while he begged Aidan to give him more time with Lukas.

I'm an actor by trade. This is just another type of stage. Aidan took a deep breath. *I have to do this.*

THE first thing Aidan realized about modeling underwear was that it was a bloody cold job. Mind you, that was to be expected, standing around in a muscle shirt and skimpy boxers. He felt horribly exposed, with nothing to distract attention from him apart from a nearby leather armchair and the crumpled white linen

of the backdrop. The rest of the room was bare except
for the camera and lighting equipment.

Sven was fussing around him. "Let me oil you
down some more, Zeb, sweetie."

"That's enough," Aidan said shortly. Sven had
already massaged up and down his arms and legs with
an enthusiasm that bordered on creepy. How the hell
did Zeb cope with this invasion of his personal space?

Sven's eyes narrowed and his gaze ran up and
down Aidan's body. He frowned. "Something's just *not
right*," he said slowly.

This is it. Aidan folded his arms across his chest,
then unfolded them quickly at the sticky feeling of the
oil. He was going to be found out. Oh well, it had to
happen eventually.

"It's the lighting" came a slow drawl from beside
the armchair. Benjy leaned around his tripod and
winked at Aidan. "It's deceptive."

"You reckon?" Sven's smile reappeared. "Of
course! He looks shorter than my last session with
him, which is of course *ridiculous*. But maybe—" He
gave Aidan a coyly suggestive look. "Carrying just a
few extra *ounces* around that midriff, sweetie? Have
you been overindulging in snackettes with—" Another
coy look, this time in Dominic's direction. "—prior
engagements?"

"He looks good to me" came a bark in reply from
the back of the room. *Dominic!* "When are you going
to get on with it?"

Sven was startled into temporary silence. Benjy
chuckled. All Aidan wanted was the white curtain to
draw him back into its folds so that he couldn't be seen
anywhere this side of the Arctic Circle.

"Of course, yes, let's get going." Sven blustered his way back behind the cameras. "If you can just run through the poses we *suggested*, sweetie."

Oh God. Poses?

For a few more seconds, Aidan stood like a porcelain statue, until Sven started calling out what he wanted. Aidan had to crouch, to reach back over his shoulder, to lift his arms behind his head.

Sven wasn't smiling any more. Aidan knew he wasn't making the grade. He'd never really considered what Zeb actually *did*, but modeling appeared to take a lot more than standing around and looking… well, just looking like yourself.

"The arms, sweetie, the *arms*." Sven was starting to look frazzled. "Turn with that clenched fist thing you do. Okay, let's work on that *chair*!"

Oh God. Aidan wondered how many times he would think that before he said it out loud and ran screaming from the room. Zeb would have to forgive him, because this was mortifying. His body had been plonked into place like a shop dummy and his limbs molded into odd shapes like kid's modeling clay. This had gone beyond sibling love and into the realms of torture; he really couldn't take any more—!

"And off with the *shirt*, sweetie," Sven called.

And double God.

Aidan peeled off the muscle vest and leaned on the arm of the chair. His muscles felt stiff and the leather squeaked as it took his weight. His nipples, suddenly exposed to the cooler air, pebbled. Out of the corner of his eye, he saw Dominic move nearer.

"Give me some attitude," Benjy said to Aidan. His camera clicked frequently in the otherwise quiet room. "You know? Your usual sassy look."

Aidan was close to frozen now. He probably looked more like a rabbit in headlights than a sexy supermodel. What sort of *look* did Benjy mean? Dominic had moved behind the spotlight by now, near enough to catch Aidan's eye.

And then Dominic winked at him.

Winked!

"Wait a minute," Aidan blurted out.

Sven sashayed up with the bottle of oil, an expectant look on his face.

"No!" Aidan snapped. He had no idea he had such an assertive tone in his portfolio, but if Sven thought he was going to lather any more of that stuff on Aidan's chest, he had another think coming.

Sven winced, held up a hand in appeasement, and backed away.

"He's fine, Sven," Benjy called over. And then, so quietly that maybe only Aidan could hear him, he murmured, "Relax. I've got your back."

Aidan, distracted by Sven flouncing around the pile of discarded and potential outfits, had no time to wonder what that meant.

"Time to change into the *blue*," Sven announced.

"What?"

"Slip off the white. Let's see the blue. You look paler than usual today, sweetie, and it'll look better against your skin."

Aidan glanced down at the blue briefs on the floor behind the chair. No, he hadn't misremembered how skimpy they were. "Don't you think this is enough?" he asked as bravely as he could. Straightening up, he caught a small frown on Benjy's face.

"Not like you to mind about stripping off," the photographer said.

Okay. Aidan took a deep breath, fought back his blushes, and pushed down the white boxers to his ankles. A quick step out of them, then a grab for the blue pair. He fumbled as he tried to pull them on too quickly, and had to take a step forward to balance himself against the armchair. It was a stretch across the floor and meanwhile everything was swinging between his legs. *Oh God, oh my God!*

"Time to update your manscaping, sweetie," Sven murmured rather acidly.

Aidan suspected Sven was still piqued at missing out on the oiling-down. He crouched down quickly, worried he could still hear the camera clicking away. Hopefully it was just his paranoia. When he yanked up the blue briefs—which were horribly shallow and he had to tuck his dick half under his balls to fit it in—and spun around, he found no one staring. It must just be normal life to these guys. Silly of him to think anyone would be watching him get his kit off.

And then he caught Dominic's gaze again.

Dominic's eyes were hot, the pupils dilated and the edges a little pink as if they genuinely steamed. The look in them was unmistakable. He wanted Aidan, and he wanted him back at the naked in-between-briefs stage. *Now.*

"Yes," Benjy murmured to Aidan, just as quietly as before. His camera clicked away. "That's the right look at last."

Dominic moved around to the side of the chair. He was out of shot, but facing Aidan. Aidan couldn't take his eyes off Dominic's face, where desire was written in every pore. Aidan wondered if Dominic could see he felt the same; that in a minute, if Dominic kept giving him *that look*, the blue briefs wouldn't have room for even Aidan's modest tackle.

Then Dominic slowly ran his finger across the top of the chair's leather back. A shiver ran across Aidan's skin like a gust of fresh, spring air, and he let out the smallest of gasps.

"Oh yes." Benjy gave a small sigh. "Perfect. That'll do it."

"It's a *wrap*!" Sven trilled with glee. "Thanks, everyone!"

Chapter Twenty

DOM couldn't remember ever feeling such turmoil. On a physical level, Zeb's shoot had wound him up into such a state of need that his whole belly ached with lust. He wanted to take Zeb to bed, and *now*. He wanted more of the kisses they'd been practicing to a very fine degree recently. He wanted Zeb in that same stage of undress, but in private and under Dom's own hands.

He fixed his gaze doggedly on the door of the changing room where Zeb had vanished to, wary that Zeb might emerge unexpectedly and escape Dom's attention, even for a second.

Zeb finally stumbled out of the closet, fully dressed now but looking a little disoriented, and Dom all but grabbed his hand to bring him close. Zeb blinked up at him with that sexy open-eyed look he had. Dom really—*really*—hoped they were on the same page on this need thing. He wasn't known for sweet-talking seduction, though for Zeb, he'd do his damnedest.

He'd do a lot for Zeb, he realized with a shiver of shock.

"Do you want to see the *shots*, sweeties?" Sven had sidled up beside Dom, as if he imagined Dom had the remotest interest in him and whatever he was gabbling about now. "Zeb likes to look *all* through them after a shoot—"

"Not now. He's busy," Dom said abruptly. "Needed elsewhere. He has to leave now." He put his hand in the small of Zeb's back. The skin felt warm, and Dom's palm was the perfect fit.

Sven looked too scared by Dom's fierceness to question the nonsense of all that, and he kept well back as they crossed the studio to the door.

Benjy met them there, flicking through the shots on his camera. "They're good."

"Good?" Behind them, Sven sounded unconvinced.

"Yeah. Not the familiar edge, I admit. But there's depth and emotion to this that's much more powerful." Benjy held Zeb's gaze for a long moment. "I'll make sure you look right every time, punk. Whoever you are."

"Whoever—?" Zeb went very still.

Benjy laughed. "However. I said '*however* you are.' I'm here for you."

Zeb laughed too, though shakily. "Thanks."

"And you look pretty tasty in the blue." Benjy's mischievous look returned, this time cast in Dom's direction. "Here. For you two." He slid a small item into the front pocket of Dominic's jeans, then went back to the cameras.

Zeb tugged on Dom's sleeve. "Let's go," he hissed. "And quickly! If Sven says sweetie one more time, I won't be responsible for the violence."

They almost ran down the stairs, chuckling. No one and nothing distracted them as they came out onto the street. If anyone did, Dom had every intention of smacking them on the nose as he had the reporter.

"Do you have your car?" Zeb asked.

Dom stared at him. *Car? What car?* He couldn't think straight. All he could see was the vision of Zeb twisting and smiling and damn near nude, apart from those bloody ridiculous blue trunks. It was as if the memory had been burned onto his mind's eye, making him feel simultaneously too hot and too cold, so he opened his mouth and let the nonsense out in a burst of his trademark honesty. "He was right. That photographer bloke. You do look tasty in blue."

Zeb laughed.

The sound was slightly nervous but still completely, utterly charming to Dom. "But even better out of it," he said huskily.

Zeb blinked rather faster than before. "Really?"

"Really." Dom cleared his throat. There were too many bloody people on the street, but that wasn't going to stop him asking. Ridiculous that he should feel so nervous! "I don't force myself on anyone, but if you don't want the next step, you'll have to take yourself out of my physical reach. I want us to go back to my place, right away. I'm not good at the pretty speeches or romantic gestures… but I want you. I don't mean in a cruel or angry way, I only want what you want to give. But I won't be responsible for my actions otherwise."

"Dominic?"

Dom loved the way Zeb always gave him his full name. Sexy as hell—the same as how he looked so serious sometimes, and how he enjoyed his food so enthusiastically, and discussed the movies they'd been to, and allowed Dom's sweeping generalization that all reality TV shows were crap, and agreed with him about the quality and sweetness of the air on the top of the hills—and especially sexy was the wicked smile on Zeb's face right now.

"That's the most romantic thing I've heard for a long time," Zeb said breathlessly. "So let's go back to yours now, right?"

DOM drove as carefully as he could. Thank God there were no accidents at Regent's Park or roadworks at Paddington. Or, God forbid, any parties of schoolkids, suicidal cyclists, or bumbling pensioner drivers to get in his way. All he could think about—hear, feel, smell sitting next to him in the car—was Zeb.

They didn't speak or comment for the whole of the journey, but to Dom's delight, Zeb seemed as aware of him in return. Every time Dom swung the car around a right-hand turn, Zeb nudged up against him. At one point Zeb put a hand on Dom's knee and didn't remove it for several minutes. Dom could smell Zeb's distinctive citrus cologne and hear his shallow breathing. The air felt too thin to him and his heartbeat was racing. He felt everything inside him quicken, exactly as if he were on top of a mountain.

The fates smiled on him. There was a parking meter right outside his house, no sign of any paparazzi, and even a patch of blue sky settling over the whole street. Maybe he'd imagined the blue sky, because he couldn't actually take his eyes off Zeb and his mischievous smile.

The key to his front door stuck for a few frustrating seconds, and then they both stepped into the house chuckling, virtually on each other's heels.

It all ground to an awkward halt.

Dom and Zeb paused in the hallway, staring at each other. They were a little out of breath, though neither had run anywhere. Dom slipped off his coat and hung it on the hook by the door. Zeb just stood there, tugging at the hem of his denim jacket. Dom couldn't help noticing it was a very restrained style, unlike some of the stuff he'd seen Zeb wear. In fact, recently Zeb looked a lot less like the fashion model Dom had first met, and much more like… just a bloke. Admittedly a bloody good-looking bloke: a witty, sassy, clever, principled bloke. A bloke who had somehow entangled himself so far into Dom's psyche that Zeb only had to gaze up into his face, and Dom's prick started pushing for release inside his trousers.

A bloke in blue briefs. Dom wondered for a wild, shameful second whether Zeb was still wearing them, or whether he'd changed back into something more respectable. *Respectable. Huh.* Dom was the one imagining his date spread out on the bed, laughing and flushed and stark naked. He was the dirty old pervert.

"Dominic?" Zeb was peering at him, a worried look on his face. "Shit. I understand. Too fast, right? Or maybe it's not the same now we're back here. You know, away from the glamor."

"What?" And God, did that come out like a bark!

Zeb shrugged very gently, his gaze skittering away from Dom's. "I'll make my way out, no problem at all.

Sorry you had to sit through all that crap at the studio.
I never expected—"

"*What*?" Dom repeated. The panic was a physical
lump in his throat. He tried to tone down his volume.
"I mean, no, I'm not sorry at all. And don't go. Please.
Don't go."

"You looked upset…."

"Everything's fine. Everything's good. Very good."
Why the hell was his expensively educated vocabulary
failing him now? He might not be the softest speaker on
the planet, but he could usually express his wants and
needs without scaring the horses.

Zeb gave one of those wicked little smiles he had,
the ones that made the back of Dom's neck tingle. "I'm
glad to hear it." He reached forward and ran his hand
along Dom's forearm. It was a tentative move and
almost shy—though Dom had no idea why the confident
Zeb Z would be nervous of approaching a clumsy old
bear like him. "But we've never actually discussed this.
You know, the… intimate terms of the deal."

"Fuck the deal," Dom said as clearly as he could.
"This is just about us. Isn't it?"

"Yes, I suppose it is. I'm just… not used to this
kind of thing."

"Sex?" Dom asked bluntly, not believing Zeb for
one second. How come he was playing so coy?

"No! I mean this sudden move. So soon. So…
unexpected."

"Unwelcome?" Dom was worried that his voice
broke on the word.

Zeb's eyes widened in that semishocked way he
had when Dom raised his voice or was particularly
aggressive. Dom was just thinking irrationally,
wildly—about grading it on a scale of sexy compared

to all of Zeb's other mannerisms, when Zeb leaned even farther forward and kissed him full on the lips.

With tongue.

Plenty of it.

"No," Zeb whispered into Dom's mouth, "not at all unwelcome. Quite the opposite, in fact."

Thank you, whatever gods are above!

Dom thrust his arms around Zeb's waist and pulled him into a hug from knee to chest. Zeb snaked a hand under the hem of Dom's shirt and ran his fingernails along Dom's skin.

Dom sucked in a thick breath. "I'll take it wherever we are, believe me," he growled at Zeb. "But my bedroom's more comfortable."

Chapter Twenty-One

AIDAN had been right when he told Dominic he didn't usually do this kind of thing. But for that glorious moment in the hall, he'd drawn on the best of both himself and Zeb, and played for what he wanted. And oh God, but he wanted Dominic! The desire clenching in his gut was hot and bold, and for once Aidan wanted to follow that path. His previous experience with men had been slow, steady, and way too cautious—and even then, he'd racked up a history of startlingly bad choices. So why shouldn't he follow the Zeb path in more than clothing and attitude, and grasp some happy, strings-free sex as and when it presented itself?

A whole new me.

Aidan paused in the doorway of Dominic's very masculine bedroom. That wasn't really the case. He was still himself—Aidan, the one in the background, the more timid twin, a quiet, creative, deep-feeling man—but the Zeb persona was very empowering. Had the modeling shoot been that horrific, or had he secretly enjoyed flaunting himself? Maybe everyone had a show-off inside them, maybe everyone enjoyed the limelight. Was it just that some people reveled in it while others held back, feeling guilty at their perceived weakness?

"Zeb?" Dominic pressed up against his back, gentle now, his mouth at Aidan's neck, his breath heating the nape. Dominic touched his throat, then ran his fingers slowly down inside the neckline of Aidan's T-shirt. "May I?"

It was a side to Dominic that Aidan hadn't seen: this careful, solicitous behavior. Aidan knew that if he said no now, Dominic would step away. Yet Aidan had no desire to do that. He turned so he was facing Dominic, slid his hand around the back of Dominic's neck, and drew him in to a new, deep kiss. "My turn to say please."

Dominic chuckled and pulled himself out of Aidan's grip. He peeled Aidan's shirt up and over his head, letting it fall to the floor.

Aidan did the same with Dominic's shirt, letting his hands linger on the muscled torso beneath. Oh God, but Dominic was fine! Aidan flattened his palms on Dominic's pecs; the dark hairs were warm between his fingers. He stretched out his little finger and flicked a nipple—a dark brown nub on a lighter brown circle, surrounded by even more of the soft, sexy curls.

Dominic gave a moan, only half under his breath. "Ouch."

"It hurts?"

"In the best bloody way," Dominic said with a grin. "If I don't get my jeans off soon, I'll end up in hospital with dangerously trapped circulation."

"Not a good thing for a mountaineer to have, I suspect."

Dominic laughed again. His breathing was heavier than before. He gripped Aidan's shoulder with one hand and used the other to release the button and zip on his confining jeans.

Aidan quickly unzipped his own, and they got into an amusing kind of race where they both tried to get their shoes, jeans, and underwear off quickly, without tripping over each other's pile of discarded clothing.

Aidan caught Dominic's gaze running up and down Aidan's body—and his brief look of disappointment. Embarrassment washed over him in a mixture of fire and ice. Surely he wasn't *that* lacking in inches—

"You left the blue ones behind," Dom said thickly. "Pity."

Aidan's relief made his laugh too loud. "You only want me for my designer briefs, eh?"

Dominic's pupils grew so large that Aidan could barely see the brown irises around them. "No way. I want you for much more than that."

Aidan gazed at Dominic: several inches taller, many pounds heavier, definitely fitter… and just the perfect man. Dominic's torso had a fine covering of dark hair accentuating the lines of his pecs and rib cage, and his upper thighs were similarly furred. It was as if someone had scribbled over the lines of his muscles with a dark, soft pencil. The cluster of extra hair at his groin was just… extra joy. Aidan's cock thickened; his skin ached with desire.

Dominic cleared his throat. "Feel free to look all you want," he said hoarsely. "I'm happy with what I've got. But I'll cope with different expectations, if that's what *you've* got."

"Don't be daft." Aidan couldn't hold back his excitement; he was sure it was beaming out of his eyes. "You're gorgeous."

"They're not too much for you? My hairy—" He waggled his brows jokingly. "—credentials?"

Aidan laughed happily. He remembered that night at the club for all the wrong reasons, but also for some of the right ones. "I'd certainly like to enjoy them to the full. Please. Let me hold you."

They lay down on top of the very large bed. Seriously, it was almost twice the size of Aidan's own. Dominic had pulled back the sheet but neither of them climbed under it. To Aidan it was the height of decadence to be lying naked on the top of a bed in the middle of the afternoon, with light streaming in from between the open curtains. But at the same time, he gloried in it.

Dominic took longer to settle on the bed, rummaging first in the top drawer of one of a set of matching bedside tables.

"Are you looking for something specific?" Aidan asked hoarsely. He had the most perfect view of Dominic's back and buttocks, as he stretched out over the edge of the mattress.

Dom cleared his throat, scattered some items on the top of the unit, and then closed the drawer. When he rolled back to face Aidan, he was flushed. "I was just getting… I mean, I don't know what you're up for, but it's best I get things prepared."

Aidan felt a thrill run down his back like the edge of a feather. "Supplies for the expedition, Mr. Mountaineer?"

"Don't." There was a strange tug to Dominic's voice.

"Don't…?"

Dominic gave a snort of disgust. "Hell. Just me, being a touchy kind of tosser. Must've been something in the air at that bloody studio. Ignore me."

But Aidan knew what Dominic was saying. This wasn't the time for teasing, however fond, however used they were to that way of interacting. He shifted closer to Dominic and nuzzled at his shoulder. "I'm sorry," he whispered. "You're not being touchy, just sensitive. I'm nervous too."

"You?" Dominic shook his head, his expression puzzled. "Come here, then. You don't have to be nervous with me."

Aidan slid into his arms, and Dominic's warmth covered him from neck to knees. Aidan's smooth skin slid against Dominic's more rugged flesh, sensuous and a little sweaty, and he wrapped his much skinnier legs around Dominic's, trying to get as close as possible.

"God. You feel… astonishing. Marvelous." Dominic's voice was ragged and he ground his hips into Aidan's, rubbing their cocks against each other.

His heart racing and his mouth dry, Aidan sat up again. He took the opportunity to run his hands down Dominic's body from the heavy, firm shoulders to his softer belly, snagging the hairs that thickened below that. Dominic's cock was heavy, lifting up from his groin. The tip glistened with moisture.

A rush of desire swam through Aidan and, scooting down on the bed, he dipped quickly to lap at it. Dominic's thighs tensed up momentarily, then his legs relaxed and fell open wider. Aidan snuggled into the harbor they made on either side of his shoulders and slid his mouth farther down the shaft.

"Oh fuck." Dominic groaned louder.

Aidan anchored his hands on Dominic's hips and began to lick up and down in earnest. He might have been a poor judge of his boyfriends' integrity in the past, but he'd always been good at the sexual part of relationships. He'd just never had much chance to relax emotionally into one. But here he was, dropping any inhibitions he'd ever had, and loving it. Dominic's limbs were strong and muscled under his grip, and the hairs on his thighs tickled Aidan's chin as he dipped deeper on Dominic's cock. When Aidan paused on an upward stroke to suck around the tip, Dominic yelped with pleasure and hovered his hand over Aidan's head as if longing to take hold of his hair but afraid to take liberties. Dominic stretched his knees even wider apart.

Aidan had been ready to roll over and take whatever Dominic wanted to give, but something about his response made him pause. He let Dominic's cock slide slowly off his tongue and sat up on his heels. "You okay?" he murmured.

Dominic raised his eyebrows. He'd gritted his teeth, as if to restrain his moans and groans. "What is it they say? Do bears shit in the woods?"

Aidan grinned. "Will you turn over? I want to see that arse of yours. I want to get my hands on it, massage it, touch it… slip a finger inside." His fingertips tingled with the need to caress Dominic all over, inside and out. "If you'd like that."

Dominic gave out another couple of gargled words that sounded like "bears" and "woods" and rolled over swiftly onto his front. Their legs tangled briefly, and then Dominic resettled himself so he was lying between Aidan's thighs.

His arse was compact for such a bulky man, but beautifully formed. Aidan felt he was being given his Christmas treat, months too early. He traced the dimples at the base of Dominic's spine. The skin was dusted with hair even down there. Then he ran a finger down between Dominic's taut buttocks.

"*Jesus.*"

Aidan noted how Dominic tensed up, but also how his cheek muscles then relaxed into the touch. Aidan licked the fingers of his right hand and ran them around Dominic's pucker, patting and stroking the entrance. The skin was darker, and the hairs tangled and deliciously damp with sweat. Dominic gave a long, very heartfelt sigh, and Aidan felt a wonderful, embarrassingly delicious feeling of power.

"Will you"—Dominic's neck was very flushed and he seemed to be having trouble articulating— "fuck me?"

Aidan's heartbeat suspended for one glorious moment, then started up again at double speed. "I'd love to."

It had been a long time since Aidan had topped. He really liked it, but his previous boyfriends had all assumed… well, he wasn't going to think about *them* any longer, was he? He ran his hands up Dominic's thick thighs, caressing the sensitive seam between thigh and buttock, teasing between Dominic's legs at the back of his balls. The skin along Dominic's taint seemed to shiver at Aidan's touch.

Aidan reached for a condom and lube from the supplies Dominic had thoughtfully prepared.

"Go slowly," Dominic said. He'd buried his head in the pillow and his voice was indistinct.

"That's how we both want it," Aidan murmured. He slid a lubed finger inside Dominic and moved gently in and out. *God.* The channel was tight and smooth, and Aidan could only imagine what it would feel like around his cock.

Dominic reached back and grasped Aidan's leg. "Zeb?"

The name startled Aidan for a second, so far from any acting role right now. "I'm here," he murmured, choked. *I wish you could call me Aidan.*

"This is rare for me."

"Somehow I don't believe that. You're not a man who ignores his physical needs."

Dominic snorted with amusement, though it was still muffled. He turned his head to the side so that Aidan could see one of his eyes, dark with both need and anticipation. "Like *this*, I mean."

What? Aidan paused. "I'm…. God, I'm sorry. It's just… you seemed ready for it."

"I am. Believe me, I am. Whatever that reporter may think."

The rude memory lingered, nudging Aidan out of his massage. *"Who plays base camp?"*

"You're the big, butch, adventurous type, Dominic," he said softly. "I'm the frail, delicate twink. What are the poor straight people meant to think?"

"Like I give a fuck." Dominic growled, suddenly still under Aidan's caresses. "But... what do *you* think, Zeb?"

Aidan gazed down at the gorgeous body laid out beneath him. He was glad Dominic couldn't see his full face and find evidence of the pained tenderness Aidan suspected was blatantly obvious there. "Like you said, I think this is just about us, isn't it? And I can't think of anything I'm looking forward to more than fucking you."

Dom let out a long, deep breath, and Aidan could actually see the muscles across his shoulders relax. "Thank God."

No more words needed.

Aidan was very careful in pushing into Dominic, but he was steady too. Somehow he knew Dominic wouldn't appreciate any further indecision. Progress was slow—Dominic was tight—but Aidan savored every fraction of an inch until he was fully inside. "Oh," he breathed. "Oh, my God."

Dominic grunted. "No, just me."

Aidan wanted to laugh but his breath was too fragile. He was limber enough to hold himself above Dominic, and he began to move back and forth.

Dominic might have been taking the receptive role, but he was far from submissive. He shook his head and clenched at the bedclothes, and generally thrashed around with enjoyment underneath Aidan. When Aidan thrust particularly hard, Dominic arched up so vigorously he threatened to shake Aidan off.

Aidan put a firm hand on the back of Dominic's neck. "You need to keep still now," he gasped. His climax coiled deep in his groin and he couldn't hold back much longer. He wished he could—even if it was only a matter of pride—but the thrill was too much. Dominic's smell and feel and the deep, rumbling huffs of breath he made on each forward thrust were the most exciting things Aidan had ever known.

Dominic stilled.

For a sudden, shocked second, Aidan thought he'd messed everything up. Who was he, telling this bold and confident man what to do? His hand looked pale on Dominic's skin, weak against the strong muscles of Dominic's back and shoulders. How had he, Aidan, got to this stage? Dominic was used to ordering people around, to forcing nature to his will—to commanding a situation. Yet now he was lying under Aidan, and Aidan was sliding in and out of him, calling the pace for them both. Aidan faltered, losing his rhythm. Dominic was magnificent, his powerful body braced on the bed, at his most vulnerable—and to whom?

Me.

"Go on. Don't... don't stop, for God's sake." Dominic growled with what sounded like a mix of urgency and bliss. His body had relaxed and he'd stopped flailing. The firm hand had done the trick.

He wants me.

Aidan's heart swelled with new joy. He slowed a little, luxuriating in the press of flesh between them, the tightness of Dominic's arse around his cock, and the fantastic view of Dominic's muscles tightening and releasing across his back and buttocks as Aidan moved inside him.

Aidan's climax burst through him suddenly and swiftly. With a cry, he shuddered and came, gripping Dominic's shoulders fiercely. Dominic gave a strangled laugh, bucked on the mattress, and the shudder that ran through him gave witness to his own climax.

Chapter Twenty-Two

DOM rolled onto his back on the bed, feeling boneless and exhausted for the best possible reasons. *Jesus.* He wondered if he'd ever move again—or if he even cared. The physical satisfaction had somehow permeated his emotions as well. He gave a long, deep sigh. He couldn't remember the last time he felt this relaxed. And happy too. *So* happy.

How bloody odd. It'd be a weird man who didn't enjoy fabulous sex like he'd just had with Zeb... but the disturbance inside him was something more. A muscle twitched in his leg, alerting him he was lying differently from usual. "Uh. Got to get up."

"Shit. I'm too heavy, sorry." Zeb wriggled away from where he'd draped himself on Dom's left side.

"The day you're too heavy for me is the day I take up modeling," Dom said gruffly, but he couldn't help the sigh of relief as he levered himself up. Years of climbing had inevitably left him with a few twinges unless he moved carefully after exercise. "I just need to clean up and get rid of this wet spot."

He walked a little gingerly to the en suite bathroom to fetch towels for them to clean themselves off. By the time he came back, Zeb had disposed of the condom in the bedside bin and already started to strip off the sheets. The sight of Zeb, naked and bustling around the bed, made Dom's heart ache in some indefinable way. Zeb looked busy, graceful, and eminently sensible—and also unutterably gorgeous. Exciting, exotic, and yet amiably companionable. *And he fucked me.* Dom felt a shiver of pure, animal lust. He shook it off and turned to the dresser to find clean sheets, and they finished making the bed together. It was a comfortable, domestic exercise that Dom couldn't remember sharing before.

Zeb caught Dom's gaze over the mattress and smiled. *So sweet.* Then he glanced down at his clothes still on the floor.

Dom spoke quickly. "Don't dress. Not yet. I'm still enjoying the view."

Zeb blushed but returned a sly smile. "Me too. But I ought to shower."

Dom moved around to Zeb's side of the bed and pulled him into a hug and a kiss that threatened to get passionate if either of them had the energy. "Take a nap with me first? We can shower after that. The bathroom's been converted into a huge wet room a man can get lost in. Only room in the house I decorated myself." He smiled, wondering if he looked as lascivious as he felt, "Maybe you can come in with me later as my navigator."

Zeb laughed with obvious delight. "Yes please."

They pulled the top sheet over them this time, grateful for the coziness. Dom hadn't had sex that energetic for a long time, and his eyelids were drooping. He drew Zeb into his embrace, his arms surrounding Zeb, his breathing matching Zeb's. God, it felt just right.

"It was marvelous." Zeb's murmur brushed Dom's chin, as intimate as a kiss.

"God, yeah. You were great. Best thing ever." Dom couldn't hold back his yawns. "I love you."

Wait! What? He had no idea where that had come from. His heart started beating too quickly.

After a pregnant pause, Zeb whispered, "Sorry?"

He didn't raise his head, so Dom couldn't see his face.

Thank God. Dom's yawn had distorted his words, and Zeb never heard that stupid slip. "I said I loved it," Dom mumbled, yawning again, though this time more for emphasis. "Bloody loved it."

"Good." Zeb gave a soft, shaky chuckle.

He must be knackered too. Dom hugged him one more time, then let Zeb roll back to his side of the bed and relax for sleep. No one outside movies slept on top of each other, in Dom's experience, or maybe he just needed more space than other men.

Despite that, his skin felt cold without Zeb against it. He tugged the sheet around him more tightly, but it took a long time to settle. His heart thumped hard from something other than the lovemaking, long after he heard Zeb's breathing slide into sleep.

AIDAN woke slowly to find Dominic lying on his back beside him, already awake but with his eyes half-closed and a self-satisfied grin on his face. Aidan smiled and snuggled up to him. The room was darker than before, and the trees outside the window had become silhouettes against the night sky. "How long did I sleep? What time is it?"

"No bloody idea." Dominic yawned. "Do you have somewhere to go?"

"No, nowhere," Aidan said gently. "But don't you think you ought to check with me first? Seems to me you're rather too familiar with making unilateral decisions."

"Damn." Dominic let out a huff of breath and turned his head to face Aidan. There was a frown between his brows, but his eyes twinkled in the dim light. "You're right. I never thought to ask. If you do have somewhere to go, it's fine. I'll take you."

"It's okay. There's nowhere," Aidan repeated, smiling. Dominic was fabulous in bed. Not only because of his sexual prowess—*God*, Aidan had no complaints there—but also the mere presence of him on the sheets, big, buff, handsome, hairy, and just… relaxed and totally content with himself. *And me?* Aidan fervently hoped so.

"Good." Dominic stretched and the mattress rocked. "Because I don't want to take you anywhere at the moment. Probably not for many hours. Days, in fact."

"We'll need to wash. And eat."

"Of course. I can't forget you love your food. I'll order in pizza. They can deliver. I'll leave the front door open for them so we never have to leave the bed."

"Except to get the pizza and bring it upstairs?"

"Damn. There's always some logistical hiccup in my bloody plans."

Aidan laughed, delighted. He'd left his jacket downstairs with his phone in it, and Dominic didn't seem to have any electronics in his room at all—not even a digital alarm—so it was like being sheltered from the outside world. It wasn't at all a bad place to be. The last few weeks had been tense and weird, and Aidan didn't feel he'd found any escape from it until now. He glanced over the end of the mattress to where Dominic's jeans lay in a heap on the floor. "What did Benjy give you at the studio?"

Dominic shrugged lazily. "A memory stick. Probably just copies of your photos, *sweetie*." Dominic did a good impression of Sven, enough to make Aidan smile and give him a dig in the ribs.

"I suppose I ought to look at them." He assumed that'd be what Zeb would do. Would Zeb be annoyed Aidan had hijacked his photo session, or would he— far more likely—laugh at the ridiculousness of it all? Aidan leaned down and wiggled the memory stick out of the jeans pocket. "Can I use your laptop?"

"Sure."

He reached for Dominic's laptop, propped precariously on the bedside table on top of an unbalanced pile of what looked like maps and guidebooks. Aidan pulled it onto his lap, popped in the stick, and fired up the contents, which were indeed photos. He started to scroll through.

Two minutes later he paused. Without a word he pressed the lid of the laptop very firmly shut and put it back on the table.

Dominic rolled over to spoon against Aidan's side. "What's up? I thought you'd be used to this sort of thing. Let me look—"

"No!"

Dominic raised his eyebrows. "Did I ever say what a touchy little thing you are?"

"Sensitive, remember?" Aidan protested. "Not touchy, you bully."

The laptop was behind him now. *Dominic mustn't see it!* He took Dominic's head in his hands and made to kiss him again.

"Oh no you don't." Dominic had the benefit of extra strength and bulk. He just leaned over Aidan, effectively pinning him in the bed, and picked up the laptop from the table one-handed. He sat up, flipped open the lid, and focused on the photo still displayed. "Good Lord!"

Aidan fell onto his back with a sigh and threw his arm over his eyes. "It's really embarrassing. How could he?"

Dominic was scrolling through a lot more slowly than Aidan had done. "They're marvelous. You look… spectacular."

"I'm naked," Aidan muttered. "Maybe they're not full-frontals—"

"This one is," Dominic murmured, his gaze fixated. "And… oh. So is this one. *Oh.*"

"—but damn near. Benjy must have been snapping away as I got changed on set. It's outrageous."

"It's gorgeous," Dom said. "You were at a photo shoot, remember? He was photographing you all the time. You weren't hiding."

But Aidan had never imagined he'd be that exposed. God, would Benjy show these candid shots along with his others? Aidan knew Zeb did nude modeling now and then. Would everyone now see him, Aidan, in *his* full, nude glory—?

"There's a note." Dominic unfolded a slip of paper that had been wrapped around the memory stick and had fallen onto the sheet. "Benjy says these are private, just for us. He'll delete the originals."

"Just for us?"

"For fun. A kind of private pornography." Dominic glanced down his body. "It's working, too."

Aidan wasn't excited by the photographs—but he was by Dominic. And he knew the best way to distract Dominic from his concentration on Aidan's embarrassment. He pushed the laptop off Dominic's lap and swung himself over to straddle Dominic's legs instead.

"You want more?" Dominic smiled wolfishly. "Did I say you were insatiable, too?"

"No. But I always say it takes one to know one." Aidan rocked his hips slowly, rubbing his cock against Dominic's arousal until he was as fully erect.

Dominic sucked in a breath. Then, catching and holding Aidan's gaze, he licked his hand and reached down to capture both cocks in his generous palm. He jacked them together, slowly and firmly until tremors of passion rippled back up Aidan's body all the way to his scalp. "Scoot up here and let me suck you."

Aidan's reply wasn't more than a whimper. He shifted on his knees until his groin was at Dominic's chin.

Dominic licked up the underside of Aidan's cock with a very self-satisfied slurp. "Don't worry about the photos," he said, low but gentle. "They will be just for us, I promise. And I meant what I said. You look spectacular. I love them."

The photos. He means he loves the photos.

"And that's the truth. I'll always tell you that," Dominic murmured.

Aidan's balls nudged against Dominic's chin, and Dominic reached with hungry lips to guide Aidan's cock even deeper into his mouth.

I know, Aidan thought with a flash of misery. *I know* you *will.*

Chapter Twenty-Three

A FEW days later, Tanya called Dom to invite him to a meeting with the potential sponsors from We Will Survive.

"Sorry to call so early in the day," Tanya said. "Hopefully I haven't disturbed your breakfast, but the client would really like to see you both in the office by two this afternoon. It's next on my list to call Zeb—"

"No need," Dom said brusquely. "He's here right now."

"He… is?" She recovered quickly from shock; he'd always admired that in her. "So can you both make the meeting? I think we're close to a deal."

"We'll be there," Dom said and hung up.

On the other side of the bed, Zeb raised his eyebrows. "What did I say about unilateral decisions, Dominic? At least when I'm involved."

Dom didn't even protest at the criticism. Zeb had stayed over several times now. His body was slim and graceful in Dom's bed, his smile the first thing Dom saw in the morning, and his sexy laughter one of the last things Dom heard at night. "I like you being involved. You know that."

Zeb frowned. "I'm not talking about sex."

"I am."

"You always are." Zeb grinned. He pushed back the sheet and reached for Dom, running his hands down between Dom's thighs. His breath was hot on Dom's neck.

"Jesus," Dom groaned. He lay back and did the only thing he could. He surrendered.

THEY made the meeting with only five minutes to spare.

Tanya and Eric met them in the lobby.

"The client is very keen to meet you personally." Tanya's gaze flickered curiously between Dom and Zeb. "They're already here."

"Great," Dom said. "That's a positive sign, isn't it?"

Tanya blinked hard. "I'm sorry?"

Dom frowned. "I was just asking."

"I know. I mean… it caught me unawares."

"What did, for God's sake?"

"That's better." Tanya smiled wryly. "The Hartington-George bark is back. I was temporarily confused by your enthusiasm."

Eric snorted in the background.

Dom scowled and then reached over and gave Tanya a brief hug. "Thanks."

There was a sudden, shocked silence. Beside her, Eric gave a smothered laugh.

"Okay." Tanya cleared her throat. Her cheeks were very pink. "Well, let's go through, shall we?"

Tanya and Zeb went first into the conference room. Eric, sporting a barely disguised smirk, brought up the rear with Dom.

"What's up with you, squirt?" Dom asked.

"Nothing. I just heard you two lit up a certain modeling studio earlier this week."

"Dear God." Was nothing sacred? Next they'd be showing peephole videos online of Dom's bedroom. Or were they already? A chill ran up his back. That would be a step too far, even for the parasites of the modern media, wouldn't it? But Eric had moved away before Dom could give voice to his paranoia.

Tanya made the introductions. "This is Felix and Claudio, the owners of We Will Survive."

The two men were opposites in build. Claudio was lean and dark, whereas Felix was much stockier with a head of ginger hair and a beard to match, but they both had an eager, determined look, matching designer suits, and presumably a matching passion for their business. Dom had seen that drive in many men over the years, whatever the industry.

Claudio came straight over and shook both Dom's and Zeb's hands. "Thank you for seeking our sponsorship," he said. "I think you'll find the new season's range very exciting, and perfect for your Eiger expedition."

Felix was slower to offer his hand. "I'll be honest, we weren't sure at first whether to consider you." He stared rather suspiciously at Dom. "It's extremely important to us that any of our ambassadors share our principles of respect and inclusivity. You're a man of great ability and drive, but you haven't always been a favorite of the media."

"That's got nothing to do with my respect for the bloody clothes." Dom tried to hold back the snap in his voice, he really did, despite Tanya kicking him in the ankle. "I've always admired your product's commitment to both quality and utility." Wasn't that what was really important? But he took several judicious steps away from Tanya so he was out of her reach.

"You weren't out to the media before now either, were you?"

Good grief. "As I've said before, I never hid it. It's not always a political issue, and I've definitely never used it as such. It's just what I am." Was Tanya brushing dirt from her eye or threatening to weep? Damned if he was going to be anything other than frank. "But neither have I avoided the most ridiculous and offensive attention from that media while I'm out with another man who happens to be gay. I think I've done my apprenticeship." Yes, Tanya was definitely on the verge of tears. He was sorry for that, at least.

But Claudio was still smiling. "Felix is very possessive of the company's reputation, as of course we all are. But it's okay, we know your personal views and we respect you for them. Our decisions should be only about the clothes, I know, and being gay—or not— shouldn't be an issue in choosing who will promote them. But it still matters to us, where we can promote that as well. At the end of the day, we're thrilled that you're comfortable with it, and have also established a high-profile career that we can support."

"Dom's totally committed to this expedition," Tanya said. "And to your company's support."

"We're offering a substantial amount of money," Felix said dryly. "That's bound to inspire commitment."

"Shut up, you old cynic." Claudio shook his head fondly at his partner. Maybe this was regular banter between them. "I think it's more than that, isn't it, Dom?"

Dom was about to respond again when, to his astonishment, Zeb stepped up beside him and slipped his arm into Dom's.

"Yes," Zeb said quietly. "It's the most important climb of Dominic's life. It's just as important to him that he shares it with people who care that much about their own work." And he smiled up at Dom as if it were the most natural thing in the world to be at his side.

"There you are, Felix," Claudio said gently. "And that's what really matters."

WHILE Tanya and Dominic worked through some details with Felix at the board table, Aidan wandered over to the coffee and refreshments. Aidan's mouth watered at the spread on offer, but didn't think a supermodel like Zeb Z would be gorging on baked goods and cookies at the first opportunity. *More's the pity.*

After a few minutes, Claudio came to join him. "I've seen your work, Zeb. You were in our swimwear campaign last year, of course."

Aidan tensed with sudden horror. *They know Zeb…?*

"Though it was unfortunate we never got to meet you in person," Claudio continued. "I can't even remember where we were that month, we travel so often during the year. But we both think you're very good."

"Thanks. That's kind of you." Aidan swallowed hard with relief. He had to avoid exposure for a while longer. *Dominic needs this deal.*

Claudio helped himself to a large espresso, a couple of pastries, and four large chocolate chip cookies. Aidan was torn between rabid jealousy and amazement that Claudio kept a figure like his on so many calories. God, now he was starting to *think* like Zeb.

"How long have you and Dom been together?" Claudio asked between mouthfuls.

"We're… it's all rather new. At the moment we're just…. Well, you know how it is."

Claudio laughed and brushed some fallen crumbs out of his goatee. He seemed to be constantly happy, and it was infectious. "Yes, I do. He's very handsome, and full of those alpha vibes. A gruff old bear, though, isn't he?"

"Not so gruff once you know him. And not so old either," Aidan said swiftly, defensively. "There's less than ten years between us."

Claudio nodded, his eyes sparkling. Aidan felt he was being undressed in a whole different way than in the studio session. "That exploit with the photographer, though. It concerned us for a while, especially Felix. He hates controversy."

"Oh God, yes. I was afraid that wouldn't look good from your point of view. Dominic felt really bad about it. He didn't mean to hit him so hard."

Claudio raised his eyebrows. "Really?"

Aidan opened his mouth to protest again but couldn't stop the chuckle that escaped. "Well, he wasn't *that* repentant."

Surprisingly Claudio laughed too. "That's fine by us. I mean, we can't condone violence, of course, but there was enough video going around the Net to show how offensively that idiot had behaved. As a company we like to be associated with strong and sympathetic characters like Dom. And of course there was the jacket—that was a big bonus."

"The jacket?"

"Neither of you realized?" Claudio laughed again. "Dom was wearing one of our jackets that day. It's very flattering—and extra validation—that he'd chosen it personally, rather than as part of this campaign." He glanced away, distracted by his partner waving him over. "I think we're about to sign off on the finance, Zeb. It's been a pleasure meeting you. And you appear to have been a good influence on Dom."

Aidan was left to think that over while the board table was strewn with papers. The main agreement seemed to have been copied a huge number of times. Dom scowled every time he was asked to sign something yet again, and Tanya kept her arm around Eric's shoulders as if to keep both his and her excitement in check.

For the moment Aidan was forgotten and was just a spectator. He watched them as if from another planet. This was Dominic's deal, his future, his dream come true. Aidan had just been part of the game, a temporary distraction. None of it had been real.

Or had it? He recalled Dominic's touch in the early hours of the morning; his fierce kisses; his warm, furred body under Aidan's; his knees gripping Aidan's hips; his desperate, sensual, and sexual need for Aidan.

But all that had been for *Zeb*, hadn't it? Not Aidan. Dominic believed him to be Zeb, even in the dark, deep night, with laughs and moans and the thrust of desire between them, when anyone else would have been at their most vulnerable, and their most honest. Aidan didn't think he had the courage to reveal the truth to anyone, let alone to Dominic.

Judging from the sudden wave of loneliness and depression threatening to creep over him, he wondered if it even mattered anymore.

Chapter Twenty-Four

AIDAN watched as Tanya left the room to escort Claudio and Felix out of the building. Eric bounded over to the refreshments to scoop up some of the remaining pastries. Dominic was left standing by the board table, looking slightly stunned.

I should go to him. Talk to him.

He wandered over to the table and put a hand on Dominic's arm to attract his attention. "It went well? As you hoped?" He felt oddly nervous.

"Even better," Dominic replied in some awe. "They're financing a large part of the expedition, plus providing all the gear we need. For the whole team. And they've offered to promote my photographs in their stores on my return. It's a marvelous result."

"Marvelous," Aidan echoed.

Dominic turned his head sharply to stare at him. But before he could say anything more, Tanya returned, grinning and clapping her hands.

"That's it, then. Well done, everybody! We did it!"

"Did what?" Aidan was startled.

"The deal is done." Tanya gave a soft laugh. "The promotion is over. You no longer have to date this gruff old grump for the money."

"Less of the old," Dominic said. His tone confirmed the gruff description, but the expression in his eyes wasn't grumpy. It was more like confusion.

Tanya turned to Aidan and gave him a genuinely warm hug. "Thank you for all your efforts."

"It was a pleasure." What else could he say? "Do We Will Survive expect us to continue as a couple?"

Tanya was supervising Eric, who was struggling to open a bottle of champagne. "I don't know, to be honest. I think the deal is done regardless. They can't legislate who will date whom, can they?"

"Of course not," Aidan said faintly, though that had already been done to him, hadn't it? However eagerly he'd finally gone along with it.

"You were invaluable, Zeb. Thank you for softening up my old bear and showing him in a more accessible light to the public."

"Somewhat," Eric murmured, with a wink at Aidan. "There are rough edges to Dom that will never be smoothed, I reckon. Am I right?"

Aidan just stared at him until Eric frowned and looked away.

"Anyway," Tanya continued. She showed no sign of noticing any tension in the room. "I'm sure you two can work on your exit strategy while Dom's away."

"Exit strategy?" Dominic growled.

"Away?" Aidan asked.

They both spoke at the same time.

Eric chose to reply to Aidan. "Dom's plans are all set for the expedition." His face was red from his ongoing battle with the cork. "It's all gone perfectly to plan. I'm really pleased for you, Dom, you grumpy old git."

Dominic still looked a little stunned. He grabbed the bottle from Eric, gave it a sharp twist, and the cork popped out with maximum effect but minimum mess. "Exit strategy?" he repeated doggedly.

Tanya smiled winningly at him, while holding her glass out for the celebration drink. "Well, yes. I mean, you don't have to suffer the socializing now. You can get back up your precious mountains. You and Zeb as a couple obviously won't continue."

"Obviously," Aidan echoed. He didn't dare look at Dominic. "I'll get some water, if that's all right."

While he fumbled over at the refreshments, trying to keep the water jug from wobbling in his hands, he felt someone approach from behind him. *Dominic.*

"Thanks for the support," Dominic said quietly to him. "Just then, when Felix was on my back."

"Of course. I mean, no problem." Aidan took a quick sip of his water. The glass was slippery from where he'd spilled some of it over his hand. "All part of the service."

"Sorry?"

Aidan felt as if he were sliding down the muddy sides of a pothole, down and down, farther into mess and misery. Yet he couldn't keep his stupid mouth shut. "My job. To make sure you gave a good impression."

Dominic was silent for a long moment. "I suppose I needed all the help I could get."

"No," Aidan snapped. "No, you didn't. You're fine as you are. And it wasn't just because of that."

"I'm glad to hear it." Dom looked pained. "I think."

"I mean—"

Dom put his hand on Aidan's arm. "Don't say any more. It's not necessary. I know what you mean."

But did he? And did he even care? Aidan felt wretched. "So, as Tanya said, the plans are all in place for the trip."

"Yes. I'll be flying out to Switzerland soon. Next Monday we start training and acclimatization in Chamonix, and then we'll do the Eiger climb over the course of three days."

Aidan's heart plummeted. *Next Monday?* That was only four days ahead. "Chamonix?"

"That's where we make our training climbs, meet the guides, establish the best approach for the current conditions. Just preclimbing fitness stuff, you know."

Aidan didn't. "More fabulous scenery, I assume?"

Dominic smiled eagerly. "My God, yes." There was a light in his eyes that Aidan had only ever seen when he talked about the mountains. "The rock face is steep and the ice solid in parts. But it's spectacular! Scrambling over the rock with an ice pick and crampons—it's totally exhilarating. It's critical to keep ourselves well hydrated and regulate our temperatures. We'll be carrying heavy packs." He focused back on Aidan, his eyes still shining. "It'd be fantastic to walk some of the peaks with you. There are smaller, easier climbs in Chamonix's Triangle du Tacul, or we could train you up on the Scottish Grade 6 pitches first. I'd love to show you…." His words tailed off. The light in his face seemed to fade. "Anyway, you're not interested in all this now."

God, did that hurt. Aidan just managed to nod tightly. "Of course, I understand. I'd still like…. I'll be following your progress—"

"On the television? Yes, I expect they'll have reporters even out there. They'll have a bloody livestream strapped to my nose if they have their way."

"And branded with We Will Survive's logo," Aidan added. They laughed awkwardly, and then silence fell again. "And when you get back?"

"Well, I'm sure we'll see each other then. Won't we?" The carefully neutral look on Dominic's face was as painful as if he'd been scowling.

"I suppose so. We'd better not stop being friends just like that. Though sometimes I think the press enjoy the romantic fights more than—"

"The happy endings, yes." Dominic seemed to tense up beside him, and not in a comfortable way. How could they feel so far apart when that very morning they'd been so close? Dominic added, "Being friends, you said?"

Aidan nodded. That was so far away from what he really wanted that he didn't trust himself to speak.

"Fine," he heard Dominic say, from what felt like a long distance. "Well, I'd better check in with Tanya before she gets too pissed to make arrangements for my money." He paused for another moment. "Thanks," he said softly. Then he turned away to join the rest of his team.

Was that comment based in anger, disappointment, or genuine care? Aidan didn't know.

He didn't think he dared find out.

AIDAN insisted on getting a cab home, even though Eric offered to drive him. He'd so far managed to keep

Dominic and his team away from where he lived, and he didn't want that part of the deception exposed. Also, he couldn't face one more minute with Dominic or his wonderful success. The man he adored every second with had become someone whose presence caused such pain that Aidan just wanted to get home and nurse his wounds in private.

As he stood on the curb waiting to hail a cab, his phone rang. At the sight of Zeb's number, he darted in under a café awning and answered the call. "Hi. How are things going?"

"Hi, bro. Things are good, that's why I'm calling. We're coming back in a week or so."

"That's great." Even Aidan could hear how his flat tone didn't match the words. "How's Lukas?"

"Lukas is fine. The surgery went well."

"Surgery? Jesus, you never said anything about—"

"Look, he wouldn't let me tell anyone." Zeb's voice was tight. "And it seems he hasn't been honest about his symptoms before now. He was at potential danger stage before anyone knew. Anyway, we caught it early, and it was a minor operation, but he's been restricted to bed rest for the time being and has promised to continue to recover at home. But are *you* okay?"

"Me?" Aidan was startled. "Yes, of course I am. Just send him my regards, and I hope you both get back here soon."

"He really appreciates you holding the fort, Ade. We both do."

Aidan wondered if Zeb realized the note of loving protectiveness that crept into his voice on the word "we." Normally he would have teased Zeb about it, but... maybe not now. A decent love affair for Zeb was long overdue. *For us all, unfortunately.*

"It's good to talk to you, Ade." Zeb laughed. He sounded more like his usual self. "I miss you."

"Ditto."

"And how's it going with H-G?"

Aidan glanced around at the other café patrons, just in case one of them got bored with their cappuccino and decided to listen in. But then… what did it matter now? "Fine."

"He hasn't been too much of a bully?"

"No. Not at all. And I don't think you should call him H-G any longer."

"Wow. Who's that assertive new guy and what did you do with my brother Aidan?"

"Ha-bloody-ha. Maybe acting the part of the outrageous supermodel is rubbing off on me."

Zeb laughed again. "About time, I'd say."

"Well, it's partly due to being with Dominic as well. He slips into Mr. Aggressive mode too easily, so I have to keep an eye on that." There was a brief moment of silence, when Aidan cursed the fact—too late to do anything about it—that he'd let slip too much passion in that statement. Zeb knew him as well as Aidan knew Zeb. "I mean, someone has to," he added lamely.

"Ade?"

"Anyway, it's all over now. He has his deal, he's off up the Eiger, and I… *you're* off the hook."

"Bro—"

"And to be honest," Aidan gabbled on, trying perhaps to cover up his lapse into overfamiliarity with Dominic. "I'm not that keen on this 'bro' thing all the time, you know? It's like we're in a buddy movie, and that's not really us. Not me, anyway. I'd prefer you just call me by my name."

There was a small but pregnant silence before Zeb spoke again. "Oh, Ade. Have you fallen for him?"

Another silence. Yes, Zeb had read the emotion beneath the random words all too well. Once again Aidan didn't trust himself to speak.

"Oh fuck," Zeb said cheerfully.

"Yes," Aidan said miserably, "I know."

"You gonna tell him?"

"What?" What a shocking thought. "Of course not. We've only been doing it for fun."

"For… doing what?"

Aidan ignored that. "He thinks I'm you. He was only doing this for the money. I'm not his type. And it's all over, didn't you hear me?"

"Got any more?"

"More…?"

"Excuses," Zeb said dryly. "Look, Ade—"

"Don't say it. I know. I'm fine." Aidan saw a cab approaching and darted out, his hand outstretched. He used the excuse of rushing to account for the wobble in his voice as he finished the call with Zeb. "Just come home soon, okay?"

Chapter Twenty-Five

DOMINIC Hartington-George was at the top of the Eiger with one of the most fantastic views in the world unfolded in front of him. He was surrounded by some of his best friends: men he would trust with his life, and often had need to. The expedition had been a great success, the weather and conditions had smiled on him, and he had some really superb photographs to document the trip.

And he felt like the loneliest man on God's bloody earth.

"Missing your girl, Dom?" joked Gerald, a lean, bald, but heavily bearded climber with years of experience and a long-term friendship with Dom.

"Man," Dom said instinctively. He barely registered the grin on Gerald's face—what he could see of it under the bundle of mask and scarf.

"Aha! A *new* man, I assume? Never seen you mooching around after someone before."

"I don't bloody mooch," Dom said, again instinctively.

"Of course not. After all, you're way past that, old man."

"Fuck off," Dom said, this time quite cheerfully.

He and Gerald laughed together. The two of them had stepped off to one side away from the main group, ostensibly for Dom to take more photos, but also to savor the successful conclusion of the climb. For a while they just stood there, companionably silent, admiring both the view and their privileged situation. The air was icy, but the light was wonderfully bright and clear. The snow covering the rock face crunched under Dom's boots as he crouched and stretched to take some more informal shots. Gerald just watched him work. They'd known each other a long time, and Dom was glad Gerald knew when to leave a topic alone.

"Good climbing equipment," Gerald said casually, as if they were discussing the morning's weather, rather than the superb quality gear that had helped them to this achievement. "Clothes too. You did well there, old son."

"They're a good company. Decent guys running it too," Dom said absently. "But yes, it made all the difference. Dad would've appreciated the same kind of quality in his day."

Gerald shifted carefully, leaning on his stick. He didn't meet Dom's eyes. "Your dad didn't make it to the top here, you know."

Dom frowned. "Of course he bloody did. I read his book. I listened to his stories. I lived in the same bloody house!"

"Steady on."

"Why did you say such a stupid-arse thing?"

Gerald sighed. "Just to provoke you, obviously."

"No." Dom parked his outrage. This place and time was too awesome for him to fall out with one of his best friends. "Sorry, man. You caught me unawares. Tell me what you meant. I can take it."

Gerald looked unconvinced but continued. "He was on the trip, definitely. But he got sick just before the final ascent. Some kind of vicious stomach bug that wiped him out, and he couldn't make the last crux. The climb was relatively short and not too steep, and he argued a long time that he could do it. But they'd left it too late in the season, the ice was dangerously smooth, and water was already running down it. He may not have had the strength to keep up—it would've been lunacy for him to try and fail."

Dom was truly stunned. He'd never heard any of this from either his father or his mother. "And you know this how?"

"I have other friends, Dom, not just you." Gerald said it with a smile to take the sting out. "Some of them related to other climbers in the original team."

"Good God." Gerald didn't volunteer any more information, and Dom wasn't sure he wanted any. All he knew was that he'd just surpassed his father in more than footsteps. He'd actually achieved more as a climber.

Does it matter? He shocked himself with the thought. Dom had been driven for so long to reproduce— and improve on—his father's achievements, only to find that he didn't experience the fierce sense of victory he'd expected when he did.

"Crafty old bugger," he muttered. "I'd never have known it from his account of the climb."

"You're not upset? Mad at him?" Gerald looked wary.

Am I? Dom didn't think so. And that was another shock, wasn't it? He'd been wedded to that resentment for far too many years. For some reason things had changed recently, and Dom's emotions and motives had moved on. Mellowed, in fact: not a word he would ever have associated with the Hartington-George menfolk before now.

For some reason? Now he was being both naive and dishonest. He knew damn well what had changed in his life in the last few weeks: something—or someone—that had shown him there was much more to existence than just his beloved climbing.

"Jesus, Ger. There are too many other reasons for me to be mad at him to need another one. And it doesn't matter really, does it? He was the same man in the end."

"Of course it doesn't matter. The team achievement remains. And your dad was perfectly entitled to write about conquering the mountain, even if he never stood on the top himself."

Dom turned to face Gerald fully, the wind biting into his face. "Why didn't you tell me before now?"

"I don't know. Well, I suppose I wondered how far your rivalry would take you. And then you've been so different this climb… distracted, I'd say."

"Yes, I have been. You're right."

Gerald looked almost as startled as Tanya had when Dom hugged her. "Who are you, and what have you done with my rude, unapologetic bastard of a friend?"

Dom winced. "Shut up. I can still take you on, Ger, and thrash you where you stand."

"You can try, you great bully. But not right now, we'd cause an avalanche." Gerald laughed and clasped Dom's hand. "I'm glad, you know? Your life's your own, Dom. You've got your own path to take, and I wanted to let you know you've done it. I mean, it's great you honor his legacy—"

"Only his climbing legacy," Dom interrupted.

"Really? No other?"

"No," Dom said more quietly. "He was my father, and so there's always respect and love when I think of him, however twisted it is with resentment and some pain. But I don't want to live the rest of my life like him."

Gerald nodded. "So that's good. The job's done. You can go back home, tell the usual mad stories at the pub, do what you want with your photos, be your own man." Gerald took a sly look at Dom. "*Get* your own man too."

"Ah," Dom said. "Well. About that."

"For God's sake!" Gerald clapped Dom's shoulder with a little too much force. "Don't tell me you've fucked *that* up, old man?"

Dom didn't want to blush. He really didn't. But he still did. "We… it was a casual thing, at least to start with. No promises."

"And?"

Bloody Gerald was relentless. When had he, Dom, ever given Gerald such grief about *his* love life? Of course Gerald had been married—and divorced—three times, with a brood of children of a variety of ages, so he was probably somewhat more qualified to preach than Dom. "It ran its course, that's all. Just before I came away on the climb."

"Bollocks!" Gerald said cheerfully and so loudly that the rest of the team glanced over their way in alarm. "You wouldn't be brooding like this if it was over. Who dumped whom?"

Dom shook his head. "It wasn't like that. We... kind of... parted."

"Kind of? When was Dom Hartington-George ever heard waffling phrases like 'kind of'?"

"Fuck off." But Dom knew his protest was halfhearted.

Had Zeb dumped him? He couldn't remember Zeb actually saying so, apart from that shitty comment about "all part of the service." Or had Dom been too quick to misunderstand? Had he dumped Zeb, purely by being so wrapped up in his bloody sponsorship deal? It had just been implied that the end of the campaign meant the end of Dom's socialization. The end of their public dating. But the look on Zeb's face when Tanya had gone blathering on about exit strategies... when Dom had said he was leaving within the week....

All he knew for a fact was that they hadn't seen each other since that day in Tanya's office. "I'm not sure he's mine. I'm not sure he wants to be."

Gerald laughed, though not unkindly. "Well, I wouldn't be surprised. You drink like a fish—and one with expensive tastes. You don't know how to give a compliment, you've never had much dress sense outside long johns, and your farts are legendary. I can't imagine who the hell would put up with that."

"I'm not all bad."

"No." Gerald grinned broadly. "You stupid pillock, I'm joking. You're loyal and witty and bloody hardworking. And you don't take shit from anyone. Your standards are the hardest I've ever had to face up to. But I appreciate that honesty and that openness."

His expression softened. "You're a bloody good friend, Dom. Any man would be lucky to have you."

"It's the other way around," Dom said morosely. "I'd be lucky to have him. If I got the chance."

"Oh, shut up with your whining, and let's start preparing for the descent. The sooner we pack up, the sooner you get back to sea level and recapturing your moochworthy boy, right?"

And Gerald took him by the shoulders, turned him around, and pushed him firmly back toward the camp.

Chapter Twenty-Six

AIDAN couldn't settle. He paced the floor of his living room, muttering, back and forth, again and again, with a copy of his new script crumpled up in his fist.

"Do you think it's early-onset dementia?" Titus muttered from his usual place on Aidan's sofa. His generous body took up two of the three narrow cushions, leaving little room for anyone else, though Simon had managed to squeeze in beside him. Titus also had a copy of the script and a pair of flimsy cherry-red reading glasses perched on the end of his patrician nose.

"Is he reading from the script?" Wendy asked doubtfully from her seat on the armchair. "I wasn't aware of any angsty teenage characters."

"He's in love," Simon said.

Aidan continued pacing, but Wendy and Titus turned to Simon in surprise. There was no surprise in Simon's adoring stare in return, totally focused on Titus.

"Give me my glasses back," Wendy said, leaning over the coffee table and snatching them off Titus's nose. "This is something I must see."

"I admit our young Shakespeare hasn't seemed himself for weeks. Why hasn't he told us he's courting?"

"It hasn't gone so well in the past, Titus. Least said, soonest mended and all that."

"Bloody nonsense! Gather ye rosebuds while ye may, is what I say." Titus and Wendy often had these quotation banters. "But he's been busy on the play, hasn't he? When's he had the chance to eye anyone up? Or be eyed up, for that matter. Has he been cruising bars?"

Wendy gave a slight shudder. "Unlikely, when I have to drag him out for coffee and cake, else he'd surely starve."

Aidan rolled his eyes. Couldn't people just leave him alone to suffer? It didn't look like the Dreamweavers were going to let up anytime soon, though.

"Who could it be?" Titus wondered, both aloud and loudly. "The postman? That simpering fool at the dry cleaner's?"

"There's been an embarrassing increase in attention when we're out in town, you know." Wendy tilted her head, appraising Aidan. "And most of it's directed at your boy Aidan."

"He gives out a very assertive air nowadays," Titus said pompously. "It's like dogs scenting the pack alpha."

"He won't thank you for that analogy," Wendy smirked.

"And I am still in the room," Aidan snapped.

"At last the wordsmith remembers us!" boomed Titus, totally unfazed.

"Temper, temper," Wendy murmured.

Simon, who'd been silent while all this was going on, shifted on the sofa and accidentally nudged a book on the coffee table with his foot. It was a large glossy hardback, and its *thump* as it fell onto the floor startled them all.

"Be careful of that!" Aidan cried. Then he sank into the armchair and put his head in his hands. He could feel the other three staring at him. Through his fingers he could see Wendy quietly pick up the book as if to return it to the table, but instead she sat with it on her lap for a while.

"Aidan, darling, it's only because we care about you and hate to see you unhappy."

"I know. I'm sorry." And he was. It wasn't the Dreamweavers' fault he'd messed up potentially the best thing in his life for the sake of... what? A game? Paying the gas bill? Sibling loyalty? "But you can't do anything about it. No one can."

"The boy feels the pain. He's been in love before," Titus said with a sigh.

"But never with anyone worth his while," Wendy said sadly.

"He needs a man with some bloody spirit," Titus said baldly. "Not one of these weedy types with floppy headgear and saggy jeans. 'Costly thy habit as thy purse can buy, But not express'd in fancy—rich, not gaudy; For the apparel oft proclaims the man.' Clothes maketh the man, as our Shakespeare's namesake says."

"But that's what I did," Aidan said softly. The pompous quote couldn't have been more apt for the mess he'd got himself into. Couldn't have been more accusing!

"Pardon?"

"I put someone else's apparel on. I let the clothes proclaim the man I was—or perhaps, if I'm honest, the man I'd like to be. But for all the wrong bloody reasons!"

Wendy glanced at Titus, who frowned in bemusement, then back at Aidan. "We don't understand what you're talking about, darling," she said.

"I dressed and acted as something—someone—I wasn't." He shook his head in misery. How could he *expect* them to understand? He didn't deserve their sympathy, let alone empathy.

"Is our Shakespeare considering a new version of *Twelfth Night*? I'm not averse to a bit of cross-dressing," Titus said in a loud stage whisper and then snickered.

Simon fairly glowed with excitement beside him.

Aidan leapt to his feet. "It was all my fault. I should have been honest with him."

"The least initial deviation from the truth is multiplied later a thousandfold," Titus quoted.

"What play is that from, darling?"

"Aristotle," Simon chirped up.

Wendy and Titus both stared at him again.

"Smart boy," Titus murmured, his eyebrows raised and his curious gaze lingering on the furiously blushing young man.

"So, Aidan, is that what it is?" Wendy asked softly. "Are you in love?"

"What the hell does it matter?" Aidan cried, startling even himself. "I let him think it was all just… just… a job! And now it's all over."

"If we can hel—"

"But you're right. Oh yes, I am!" he interrupted, barely hearing Wendy's kind words. God, it was true, wasn't it? "I do love him. I miss him like *hell*. Oh God, I didn't realize. I never said. *Oh God*."

"I'm still betting on the teenage character," Wendy murmured. "He has the angst and all the speech mannerisms quite perfectly."

"You can tell us about it, kid," Titus said in an uncharacteristically gentle tone.

"No, I can't. I can't tell you any more than that. It's a horrible mess, and it's best if you just leave me be. I'll call you in the next few days to start rehearsing again."

"Now, wait a moment, Shakespeare—"

"No, we should listen to him." Wendy put out a hand to halt Titus's protest. "Aidan, darling, you know where we are if you need us." She stood, and Titus hauled himself off the sofa with Simon's eager help. Wendy still held Aidan's book in her hands. "You know, I love these coffee-table tomes," she said. "Though I had no idea you were keen on either geography or mountaineering. But it's a vicarious thrill, isn't it, darling? One can almost live the adventure with the author. It's about Makalu," she said to Titus, who was staring at her with incomprehension. "A wonderful mountain peak in Nepal, I believe."

"Fifth highest in the world," Aidan muttered under his breath. Shit, he was quoting mountaineering facts now.

"Oh, and just before I go—" At the door, Wendy turned with what Aidan knew she called her Columbo moment, probably to give him more unhelpful advice on running his love life. Then he felt guilty at being so churlish. "—there's a press conference tomorrow in Covent Garden, for that mountaineer who's just got back from the Eager."

"Eiger," Aidan corrected before he realized what he was saying.

Press conference?

Wendy stared at him, not as if she was concentrating on him, but rather as if she was trying not to catch Titus's eye. Her mouth twitched oddly. "It's at a studio very close to our agent's. Did you want to go?"

"Me? It's not a performance, Wendy. Those things are just for journalists."

"No, it's open to the public too. One of my nephews is a reporter for the *National Geographic*, and he has some VIP tickets." Aidan should have guessed there'd be a nephew involved somewhere. "What's the man's name?" she continued, musingly. "Hardly-George or something? I read his father's book about his climbing career, you know. It was fascinating. A tad arrogant, but then the man was like that in life, I believe. His son's photography is marvelous. I only hope he hasn't inherited that arrogant streak."

"He hasn't," Aidan said. And when was he going to learn to keep his mouth shut?

This time Wendy looked blatantly at Titus and winked. "You owe me a tenner," she said to her fellow actor. "I told you it was Aidan we saw in town that day with Dominic Hartington-George."

"Oh! No! Wait!" Aidan didn't know what to do or say. "It wasn't me. Well… yes. And no. It was. Wasn't."

"Good Lord," Titus groaned. "Man can't string a sentence together now. Whoever said, 'Death and life are in the power of the tongue: and they that love it shall eat the fruit thereof'?"

"Proverbs," Simon muttered, but no one was listening to him now.

"Aidan? I'll meet you outside the Tube at two tomorrow," Wendy said. Her tone brooked no argument. "We shall all go to the press conference together."

"Will there be booze?" Titus asked, but no one bothered to answer.

Chapter Twenty-Seven

"WHO the hell's coming to this thing?" Dom asked petulantly. "I don't have time for this. Can't you just show them some of my photos?"

Tanya sighed. "I see you didn't leave your antisocial behavior behind on the summit. They want to see *you*, Dom. They want to hear what it was like, ask about the whole Hartington Hike project. And"—her voice grew steely—"you want to sell the photo account, don't you? These are the people who'll do that for you."

"Reporters. Photographers. Hack writers. Ogling me like some bear in a cage."

"Never a truer word," Eric murmured, half hiding behind Tanya. "Looks like we may have to arrange another socialization session with the supermodel for our mountain man."

"What did you say?" Dom snapped, turning on him.

Eric started, eyes widening. "I just.... Dom, I didn't mean anything." And then his eyes narrowed again, as if he'd only just heard the note of fearful hope in Dom's voice. "Oh. Oh hell, so *that's* how it is."

"How what is?" Tanya asked, though she didn't pause long enough for an answer. "Dom, I need you to come along to the studio an hour or so beforehand, okay? Just so we can see to your makeup and get the audiovisual presentation working properly. You know where it is, don't you? Macklin Street's not far from here."

"Yes, I know it."

Of course he bloody did. What twist of fate had made the Stefanowicz agency—*Zeb Z's* agency—offer their photographic studio for free to Tanya's company? No matter, it probably made commercial sense. After all, they'd worked together before, were close in location, and had occasionally helped mutual clients, like Dom himself. But it didn't make bloody sense to Dom, on any level. Not that he was thinking very rationally nowadays.

It didn't mean Zeb would be anywhere around on that day. Or would want to be. Why would Zeb Z bother to come to a press conference that didn't involve *him*? He was a model; Dom was a mountaineer. Their paths had taken different routes before they met in person, and now they had again. The few weeks they'd spent together had been the exception, not the rule.

Except I want it to be the rule.

For God's sake! Dom wondered if he were suffering some kind of mental breakdown, though he had to admit he'd never felt so bloody excited and alert

to life around him. Well, most of the time. The rest of
the time he felt like crap. He'd never been in such a
volatile state. He was always restless just after a trip,
as he acclimatized to routine life at home, but this was
something much worse.

He hadn't had the courage to contact Zeb. Not
while he was away, not as soon as he got back. What
was he scared of? But the kid had been so offish at
the meeting with We Will Survive that it had thrown
Dom off balance. He thought they'd been getting along
so well, and then… it was over. So despite what he'd
confessed to Gerald in a moment of weakness on top of
a bloody mountain, Dom had decided to take the moral
high ground and insist it was no bother to him whether
he saw Zeb again or not.

And how's that going, you blithering idiot?

Tanya had wandered off to talk to staff in the next
office. Dom reckoned he had time to catch lunch at an
Italian café around the corner, then pitch on over to
the studio. No point in going home for the few hours
between appointments. Besides, whatever his mood,
and however much he complained, he wanted to show
off his pictures at their best. Tanya had arranged with
the studio to run a slideshow behind him while the
parasites—sorry, the press—asked their questions.

"Dom?" It was Eric, appearing at his elbow and
surprisingly tentative. "Sorry, old man. I didn't mean to
tread on your toes back there. I had no idea."

"About what?"

"Well. You and Zeb Z. Looks like it developed in
an unplanned way, am I right?"

Of course he bloody was. Dom just wasn't sure he
wanted it broadcast anywhere, when he'd made such an

arse of himself. "Any point in telling you to mind your own business?" he asked gruffly.

"None at all," Eric said, with a return of his usual spirit. "But any problems, and I've got your back, okay?"

DOM stood in the middle of the empty Stefanowicz modeling studio and wondered what the hell he was doing. After leaving Tanya's office, he'd decided to pass on the Italian lunch and had grabbed a quick sandwich instead. It wasn't that his nerves were affecting his stomach, but he couldn't seem to call on his usually healthy appetite. He'd therefore arrived at the studio a full two hours before Tanya was expecting him, and no one from her company had arrived yet.

A flaky little chap on reception barely managed to check Dom's name off on the visitors' list without having palpitations, and didn't seem able to tell Dom anything more about the event. Dom summoned up his most assertive tone—no problem, when the twink was quivering somewhere between abject fear and incomprehensible lust at the mere sight of him—and said he'd wait in the studio until his agent arrived. He'd let himself up the stairs to find the studio deserted as well. Later on in the afternoon, he was sure it would be full of cameras and props and rows of chairs for the visiting rabble. Probably urns of crappy coffee too. Over by the window, behind a stack of paneling, he found the leather armchair that had been part of Zeb's set that day. He hauled it out into the main area and sat himself down. It was surprisingly comfortable for a bloody prop.

God, he was in such a bad mood! It really wasn't justified. He'd just completed one of the greatest achievements of his life, and he *wanted* to share it with the public. This was all for his benefit; he forgot that too easily. It wasn't fair on Tanya and Eric, and his other friends who had to put up with his grousing.

But the last time he'd been in here... he couldn't help remembering the scene. Why shouldn't he, when it had led to him taking Zeb to bed for the first glorious time? Initially it had been a passing inconvenience to get caught up in Zeb's photo shoot, then a tease—and then something very much more. He recalled the heat that had suffused him as he saw Zeb do his stuff. Yes, it was great to see him naked; Dom wasn't denying his healthy libido. But he'd loved watching the man twist and pose, acting out the part, even though there'd been a strange reluctance in Zeb's attitude toward it all. They'd shared enough glances during the shoot for Dom to have felt they were attuned to each other, that they were getting the same kick out of it—that they felt the same way.

And what way's that, Dom, you bloody fool?

He couldn't say it aloud. It was something he'd never put it into words before, in the whole of his life. Yet he'd never considered himself a coward before either, and he found it was a strange kind of hurt.

Distant voices drifted into earshot at the bottom of the stairs, not loud enough for him to recognize, but he knew it was time to put his game face on and start the show. With a sigh, and after a brief trail of his fingers over the back of the chair, he walked back to the door to meet whoever it was.

However, they had paused down in the hallway, and Dom wasn't sure whether to call out or go down to greet them. After all, he'd probably be in the way until they wheeled him out for his actual performance. So instead he peered over the top banister, just to check whether it was Tanya.

Oh my God.

Is that Zeb? At the same time as Dom realized he'd subconsciously been hoping to see him, he also realized how unprepared he was for the emotional impact. Zeb was on the far side of the hallway, hidden by an awkwardly placed corner of the staircase. Only his left side had been in view, and for mere seconds, but the hint of his naturally graceful body had been enough to make Dom's heart jump. And there was no mistaking that bloody annoying woolly sweater he was wearing! Zeb's arm waved into view then away again, accompanying the conversation Dom couldn't hear. His movements seemed more fey than Dom remembered, but the reaction in Dom's groin was frighteningly familiar. Also the ache inside his chest.

Dom had a better view of the other person in the conversation—an older man with an air of confidence and maturity that Dom immediately respected. Maybe he was someone important in the studio hierarchy. He was handsome too, in an elder-statesman kind of way. Not Dom's type, but maybe appealing to a younger bloke. There was something about him that declared he was gay. Dom had never trusted in this *gaydar* thing that Zeb had chatted to him about sometimes. But this guy… yes. Definitely gay. And Zeb, of course, *was* a younger bloke.

Dom didn't immediately acknowledge the disturbing feeling rising up inside him. Or maybe he didn't want to put a name to it? As he watched, fascinated in a shameful, car-crash way, the older man leaned into Zeb until both their heads were out of sight.

Zeb's hand appeared on the other man's shoulder, as if drawing him in, maybe to say good-bye.

They're very close for a simple good-bye. Dom felt his teeth clench. *Too bloody close.*

The older man's body pressed closer to Zeb. Dom could recognize the angle of a kiss as well as any other man, and it didn't look like it was on the cheek. A deep kiss. A long one.

Presumably not a closed-mouth event either.

Dom didn't know what to think. Well, yes, *fuck*, he did know what to think. Either Zeb had moved his love life on with alarming speed while Dom was away, or… he'd been with this bloke all the time. Their conversation had been relaxed, speaking of long familiarity. The older man had smiled at Zeb and moved in for a clinch far too easily for Dom's liking. Looked like they were old friends.

Or old lovers.

Dom's boot accidentally kicked the edge of the banister and the wood creaked loudly. He froze in place, still leaning over the rail in full view.

Downstairs in the hallway, the older man lifted his head, his gaze seeking the source of the noise. There was movement under the staircase as Zeb peeked out of his shelter. Dom was scrambling to move away from the banister, but he still caught a glimpse of the expression on Zeb's face. A frown of puzzlement. Then a look of unmistakable recognition and total, horrified shock.

Several things happened at once. Zeb opened his mouth as if to call up to Dom, and Dom jerked back against the wall of the landing. The front door banged open and Tanya marched into the hall, calling a cheery hello. His name was mentioned, both by a male voice and by hers.

"Dom?" she called up the stairs.

"You there, old man?"

Tanya *and* Eric. Dom backed away to the studio, his escape route cut off. The front door banged again; maybe Zeb and his companion had left. Eric came thundering up the steps and Tanya's lighter footsteps followed.

"No point hiding up here, Dom!" Eric crowed. "The crew are on their way. Fifteen minutes and we'll be ready for sound checks. It's nearly time to face the music, right?"

All Dom could think of was the fleeting look on Zeb's face.

Facing the music.

Right.

Chapter Twenty-Eight

"HERE," Wendy said, fussing over Aidan. "Here are some free seats. Hurry up, they're starting."

She nudged Titus none too gently into one of the uncomfortable plastic seats at the back of the studio, and pulled Aidan down onto the seat on her other side. He muttered an apology to the older woman next to him, who was dressed in a smart tweed suit and wore ostentatious pearl jewelry, and whose handbag he nearly put his foot in. There'd been an engineering problem on the local Tube line, so they'd almost missed the start of the event. As it was, the rather snotty little twink on reception had only just been persuaded—by Titus in his Henry V persona, no less—to let them in.

Aidan hadn't seen anyone on the way in apart from the twink. Even so, he'd pulled his hoodie over

his head so that his hair was hidden and his face shaded.
Ridiculous, to think that anyone would notice him, but
it felt risky when he'd been here as Zeb not so long ago.
He glanced around quickly, wondering if Zeb was back
from Switzerland yet. Since the call on the day he and
Dominic had met the men from We Will Survive, Aidan
had heard nothing more about Zeb's itinerary.

What exactly am I doing here anyway?

He wriggled awkwardly on the seat, wishing he
had something more flexible under his bum, something
more like the leather armchair that had been part of the
shoot. But really, he had no business at the Stefanowicz
studio at all now his "Zeb" time was over. This place
was for the media crowd, full of bright, bold, decisive,
extrovert young things, not him.

They were sitting at the back of the room, so
Aidan could barely see over the heads of around fifty
people, who he assumed were mostly journalists. But
he couldn't miss the semicircle of armchairs placed at
the front, with standing lights behind them. A murmur
through the crowd announced that people were filing
into the room and moving to the armchairs. Applause
rippled through the audience. Spotlights snapped on,
flooding the seats. Cameras started flashing from the
crowd in front of him.

Claudio from We Will Survive took one seat,
smiling broadly. Tanya, in a glamorous designer skirt
suit, took the next. Then a TV presenter, whom Aidan
recognized as the front man for a lot of adventure
programs, and a tall, bald, bearded man, who was built
like a brick wall and had a tanned, weather-beaten face,
sat down.

And then Dominic Hartington-George himself. The crowd clapped more loudly, though Dominic looked… how would Aidan describe it?

Uncomfortable.

Oh, but otherwise Dominic looked good. So good! He stood confidently, tall and broad in a plain blue shirt, jeans, and the jacket he'd worn the first time Aidan met him, with his curly hair a little longer than when Aidan last saw him, and his beard well trimmed. Dominic almost glowed with health, and Aidan's heartbeat started racing. Was this going to happen every time he saw the bloody man? His breathing felt tight and his lap suspiciously warm. At this rate he'd have to hide in the flat until the news stories died down. But then there'd be Dominic's book launch, and how it was the perfect gift for Christmas, so it would be all over the online bookstores. And then probably TV interviews as well, and maybe Dominic would even end up going on *I'm a Celebrity in the Jungle with a Ballroom-Dancing Quiz-Show Presenter Who Bakes in His Spare Time.* Aidan couldn't help it; he snorted a laugh out of his nose.

The smart woman in the next chair looked in surprise at him. On his other side, Wendy jabbed him in the ribs.

"Sorry," he mouthed to anyone who might see.

The interview session itself was a thrill for Aidan. He was immediately fascinated, especially when he'd heard so much about Dominic's early plans and, of course, actually been involved in steps along the way.

Firstly, Claudio spoke excitedly about his company's involvement. He described the marketing campaign with Dom's photos that would be launching in their shops over the next few months. The expedition had obviously kept in touch with him and Felix, because he was able to talk about the route with confidence.

The second speaker was the other large man. He was also a climber—Gerald someone—who'd been on the expedition with Dom.

Aidan leaned forward in his seat to hear better. He'd been following the trip in the news coverage, but that was nothing like hearing from the people who'd really been there. In the news he heard about the weather and saw some of the photos sent back to base, but as Gerald spoke, Aidan could almost imagine he felt the icy wind, and heard and smelled the crisp snow underfoot.

Gerald was very entertaining about some of the mishaps they'd had, and what remnants they had to eat when the decent stuff ran out because he'd forgotten to bring one of the packs Dom had designated for him to carry. Gerald told how they had a guide whose English was so heavily accented that his description of the ice surface as "firm" sounded like "farm," and they had continuing visions of a herd of llamas following them like sheep behind a shepherd. And one morning Gerald had gone for a piss in the snow, and because all the blood in his body was being used for the climb, when he rummaged inside his trousers all he found was a shrunken acorn shape instead of his—

The presenter tactfully interrupted and moved the conversation to Dominic.

And that was where the interview became torture to Aidan. Dominic was the center of attention: all eyes were on him. He was surprisingly charming, considering Aidan knew how much he'd be hating this. He praised and complimented his climbing team and guides, talked very civilly about his father's legacy, and thanked We Will Survive fulsomely for their support in making the whole thing happen. He was particularly grateful for the equipment they'd supplied.

"He knows not to bite the hand that feeds, eh?" Titus hissed over at Aidan.

Aidan knew it was much more than that. He recognized the zealous light in Dominic's eyes as the slideshow of his photos started up behind the chairs. Everyone's gaze immediately turned to the breathtaking view from the top of the mountain. Trust Dominic to ignore the expected, which was to begin with the planning of the expedition! Instead he'd started with the striking impact of its end. He then interspersed the more fabulous shots with fascinating insights into the team's work, the equipment they'd packed and used, the towns they'd visited on their way to the Eiger, and the people who'd been their guides and support services.

The photos were astonishing. The scenes were not just beautifully shot but presented with bold, elegant showmanship that kept the whole audience entranced. Dominic had a style all his own and an eye for drama. A couple of shots of the team packing up the kitbags seemed routine, but became a moment of shared camaraderie with a joke or two; a portrait of three men leaning into the wind became a vivid illustration of the whole team's determination and struggle.

Aidan leaned back in his chair and surrendered his heart and mind to the wonderful, theatrical experience.

AT the end of the show, several people pushed forward to shake Dominic's hand, or to quiz Gerald about the trip. Photographers took some extra portrait shots of the climbers. Dominic and Gerald looked good together, relaxed and comfortable in each other's company: two strong, capable outdoorsmen.

Aidan felt the stabbing pain of jealousy. Dominic had told him there was no romance or even sex between him and anyone on his team; that their closeness was based on friendship, trust, and love of the climb. But Aidan couldn't help but feel an outsider in Dominic's world. His head told him it would never have worked between them and he should sneak off now while he could get lost in the crowd, but his heart couldn't resist joining the queue to meet Dominic. His heart didn't *want* to resist.

"Dominic? That was marvelous. I loved hearing—" Aidan's words dried up as he caught the blank, cold look on Dominic's face.

"Thanks for coming." Dominic shook his hand as he had done all the other reporters or visitors. There was no particular warmth in it. His gaze flickered over Aidan and a slight frown creased his brow. "Glad to see you dumped that filthy sweater."

Sweater? What was he talking about?

Aidan felt nauseated at Dominic's cold-shouldered response. Surely he didn't deserve that? When Dominic turned away from him to greet another well-wisher, Aidan grabbed his arm and pulled him back around. "What's wrong?"

Dominic gave a sharp, mirthless bark of a laugh. "Don't play me for a fool."

"I'm not. I'd hoped we could at least be civil. You seem pretty glad to have moved on."

"Moved on? *Me*?" Dominic's eyes darkened. "You really want to discuss this in public?"

"Yes," Aidan said bravely. But… discuss what? Aidan couldn't bear the look of hostility on Dominic's face. What the hell was his problem? Was it because Aidan hadn't been in touch since Dominic got back? Did something go wrong on the trip or maybe with the funding? But surely Dominic couldn't blame Aidan for any of that.

Dominic gave a slow, ragged sigh. "I just think you should have told me."

"Told you what?"

"That you were seeing someone else. I know we were just a business arrangement, and we said all that crap about no strings and being seen just for the press—"

"Wait a minute. Seeing someone else? What are you talking about?"

Dominic had continued regardless. "I may be blunt, I may be antisocial, I may—occasionally—be downright rude, but I don't cheat on a lover, whether I'm with them for a week or hope it'll be much longer."

Cheat? What's happening here? Aidan, without thinking it through, got angry instead of asking outright. "I should have told you? I don't remember you *asking*! To tell you the truth, I don't remember *anyone* asking, when they wanted me to date a complete stranger for the sake of the publicity." Okay, so Zeb had asked if Aidan had a current boyfriend, but it had been a late afterthought. "Oh, and let's not forget, for the sake of the money too."

"So you want to bring that up as well?" Dominic scowled at him. "I assume you did all right out of it. Let's face it, I understand how these things work."

"These things? What *things*?"

"Deals," Dominic hissed. "Arrangements. Campaigns. Paper dates. Whatever you and your agency want to call it."

"Paper dates? What the hell does that mean?"

"You bloody know what it means. You played your part well enough, didn't you?"

"Dom?" Tanya tugged at his arm. "Claudio wants to introduce you to a production company."

But Dominic remained focused totally on Aidan. "Don't get sanctimonious about it now. You knew from the start what the terms were."

Oh God, Aidan had never known a statement prove so untrue.

"It was all false. A game." Dominic was trying to lower his voice, but his anger vibrated in every syllable. "More fool me to let it run away from that. We were both paid for it, and you were happy enough to move on as soon as I got the funding. If, in fact, you were ever free to start with. After all, we didn't see *that* much of each other. You had plenty of free time to maintain your glamorous model lifestyle. How many other men were you dallying with while you were fluttering those long eyelashes at *me*?"

Dallying? *Dallying?* "No one uses that bloody word anymore!" Aidan snapped. Why the hell was he worrying about Dominic's vocabulary rather than his vitriol? And why was Dominic being so cruel? So unfair? "I never dated anyone else at all. I can't believe you think I would have. I can't believe you have so little respect for me, after I thought we had a real connection—"

He realized that silence had suddenly fallen around him a split second after he saw Dominic's gaze focus on something over Aidan's shoulder and his mouth drop open. Everyone else facing Aidan was looking that way too. Shock registered in every expression.

"Aidan?" someone said softly behind him.

Aidan turned slowly, resignedly. Never had he been so unhappy to see his twin. Zeb was standing in the doorway of the studio in one of his trademark neon sweaters and skinny jeans. His hair was longer than usual and softened by what had obviously been weeks of professional inattention, but he was still the same old Zeb, except today his expression was solemn. "Bro."

Aidan's hood had fallen back; his hair was still styled in the same way as Zeb's. They were of a similar height and build, and no more than three feet apart. There would be no mistaking the fact they were related.

"There's two of you," Dominic said weakly. His gaze darted back to Aidan, then away to Zeb again. "Two."

"Oh my God," Tanya breathed.

"Two of you," Dominic repeated, though his gaze kept returning to Aidan. "What the hell's going on?"

"Who are you?" Wendy asked, turning her head sharply from side to side as if she were at a Wimbledon tennis match. "Either of you."

"I'm Aidan," Aidan said. "Wendy, you know who I am!"

Wendy shook her head slowly. "Darling, I thought I knew, but this is astonishing."

"And I'm Zeb," Zeb said firmly. He moved over to Aidan's side and took his hand.

Dominic's bemused voice cut in over everyone else. "You're not Zeb. How the hell can you be? Who's Aidan?"

"Aidan," Wendy said sharply. "You owe us an explanation, I think."

"Two of them? You greedy man," Gerald murmured at Dominic's side, with a broad grin. "You only told me about Zeb."

"And who the bloody hell is *Zeb*?" came Titus's booming voice from the back of the studio.

Aidan sank down into one of the armchairs and put his head in his hands.

Chapter Twenty-Nine

ZEB squeezed Aidan's shoulder. "It's time, don't you think? We need to come clean."

"We can't. You can't. *Oh fuck*." Aidan didn't know what to do, what to think. Everyone was clamoring at him for explanations, for excuses, for information. Wendy and Titus looked stunned, and the look on Dominic's face was excruciating. This was the worst day of Aidan's life.

Zeb slipped his hand away and stepped in front of Aidan's chair. "Okay. I got this poor man in trouble, so it's up to me to sort it out."

"Zeb!" The reporters started calling to him.

"Are you really Zeb Z?"

"Zeb, is he a body double?"

"Shut up," Zeb snapped. The cameras still flashed, but the journalists stopped shouting. For the first time, Aidan noticed the man who'd followed Zeb into the studio, standing quietly at the back of the crowd, watching Zeb closely.

Lukas. Aidan breathed more steadily. Did this mean there'd be some sense brought into the situation? Lukas had been the twins' rock through many turbulent times. It seemed, however, he was giving Zeb the lead on this.

"I am Zeb Z," Zeb said. "I'm not stripping anything off to prove it to you. You'll have to take my word for it. Or the word of Lukas Stefanowicz."

The cameras swerved toward Lukas, who nodded confirmation.

Zeb continued. "And this is not my body double, as you so insultingly suggested. This is my twin brother, Aidan."

"How long have you had a twin, Zeb?"

Zeb rolled his eyes. "Since birth, you moron."

The crowd laughed. "Where's he been hiding, Zeb?" shouted another reporter.

"He's not been hiding," Zeb snapped again. Aidan had rarely seen his twin so authoritative, and when he glanced across the room he saw Lukas's obvious approval. "He's been leading a perfectly normal and, I can tell you, successful life that just doesn't happen to be in the public eye. Yet." He glanced quickly at Aidan, then back to his audience. "And he doesn't need you lot harassing and bullying him. Either of us, for that matter. Remember what you're all here for, and it's not us, is it? It's for the report of this spectacular expedition, the final stop on the Hartington Hike." He swept a hand theatrically toward Dominic, as if to direct the attention of the press back to the official event.

"Decent of you to remember us," Gerald said, still grinning. "Though I'm about ready for the pub now, I can tell you. I'm happy to take new friends along with me too." He smiled down at Wendy. Somehow she'd ended up beside him and was staring up at his wolfish smile with wary admiration.

"Now wait a minute!" came a crisp cry from Tanya. "You can't just dismiss all this with a few words and a pint."

"Tanya—" Eric began.

She ignored him and turned to Aidan. "I'm not entirely sure which one you are, but I think it's disgraceful that you've deceived and manipulated us and our client."

"Tanya," Dominic said in a surprisingly mild tone.

Tanya ignored him too. "So, who have we been negotiating with? Who's been dating my Dom? Who's responsible for mellowing him to the extent I got my first hug ever?"

"For God's sake," Dominic muttered.

She glared at him. Her voice was climbing in both volume and pitch. "And who's responsible for dumping him and making him the sourest, most miserable he's ever been, since he came back from the trip?"

"Now wait a minute," Aidan protested to her. *Dominic's miserable?* He stood, tired of cowering behind Zeb's defense. "I never dumped him. You were the one who said the deal was done and the charade was over. I assumed I wasn't needed any more."

"What do you mean, you never dumped me?" Dominic's voice broke in.

DOM reckoned it was about bloody time he spoke up for himself. This whole thing was pretty bizarre, but there were certain things he'd like to get straight, in a manner of speaking. "You said, 'all part of the service,' remember? It was a clear statement that things were over."

"Oh hell, no. It wasn't… I didn't mean…" Zeb—no, Aidan—shook his head, his eyes wide. "I thought it was what *you* wanted."

"Did you say charade?" Claudio called over. Everyone seemed to have forgotten that a representative of the sponsors was still there, and one who looked very aggrieved. "Tanya, is this something we need to discuss?"

"Everything's fine," Tanya said, though she didn't look sure.

"It wasn't a charade," Aidan ground out through gritted teeth. "Nothing was a charade on my part."

"Nothing, you say?" Dom asked quietly.

Aidan met his gaze fiercely. "Nothing."

Dom couldn't mistake the sincerity in Aidan's eyes. He couldn't believe the rush of relief and excitement that suffused him. *Stupid man! Both of us. If we'd just been more honest—*

"Excuse me, but it sounds like everything has been a lie," Claudio said tartly.

"Don't be so bloody ridiculous," Dominic replied, still gazing at Aidan and ignoring Tanya's groan of despair behind him. "Are you suggesting I didn't climb the bloody mountain?"

"He did. I'll vouch for him on that," Gerald said robustly. "He snores like the dickens at high altitude. No one else reaches that particular pitch."

"Look," the real Zeb said, sounding a little panicky. "None of this is anyone's fault except mine. Why isn't anyone listening?"

"You were happy with it all? With me?" Dom asked Aidan. He had to know the real truth about his date. And not about the stupid acting-like-his-brother thing.

Aidan's eyes shone with anger, fear, distress—God only knew what else. "Yes. Oh *yes*."

"Excuse me?" Claudio repeated, his voice rising in pitch. "I need a full explanation."

"They won't ask for Dominic's funding back, will they?" Tanya muttered, probably too loudly, because Claudio winced.

Aidan turned to Claudio, his expression pure misery. "You're right in one respect. Something *was* a lie. I'm not Zeb. I never was."

"Thank God for that!" Dominic said grimly. He was pleased to see it startled them all. "Though the pair of you had me going when you appeared side by side. For a second I thought I was hallucinating. I wondered what was in that ghastly coffee."

"But you've been pretending to be Zeb?" Tanya looked close to tears.

"I don't know what to do about this," Claudio said.

"Nothing," Eric said smartly. "You signed up a gruff old mountaineer who's done you and your products proud. That's still the same, whoever he's been snogging for the gossip mags. Isn't it?"

Tanya looked close to fainting now. Dom was torn between wanting to crow and concern for her.

"No harm was meant," Aidan urged. The hostile glares had him trapped like a hunted animal, and Dom had an overwhelming urge to shield him from it all. "It wasn't meant to go that far."

"What do you mean by 'that far'?" Dominic asked.

Aidan stared at him again. A blush crept up his neck. "I'm not talking about *that*."

"About what *that*?" Dominic asked relentlessly.

"Please," Aidan hissed at him. His eyes were darting back and forth again. He looked so upset at Claudio's shock, the Lukas bloke's frown, Tanya's threatening tears, his friends' condemnation, and— dammit, probably at Dom's growling too.

Instinctively, Dom stepped toward him.

"Look!" Aidan cried desperately, apparently to everyone and anyone. "It was to help out Zeb. Just one evening, he said. Just one date, until he could take over. I didn't know I'd fall in love!"

The room fell momentarily silent.

"What?" Dom's breath felt suddenly tight in his chest.

"What the fuck?" Gerald muttered to Wendy, though loud enough that everyone could hear.

"I saw it first," Wendy muttered back to him. "Saw how bad he had it. The poor darling's been so unlucky in love in the past. We'd almost given up hope—"

"Wendy!" Aidan wailed. "Are you really airing my dirty laundry here? *Now*?"

"Please. Tell us what's really going on," Claudio said. At this point he looked more confused than angry.

"I couldn't go on the date with Dom. I had to be somewhere else," Zeb replied. He glanced at Lukas, whose expression had shifted from approval to annoyance. Zeb grimaced briefly, then continued. "I asked Aidan to take my place so that we didn't break the contract."

"You see," Aidan added, "no one would tell the difference—"

"Well," Dom interrupted very loudly. "That's the first thing I take serious issue with."

"You… what?" Zeb asked.

"But we're identical twins." Aidan stood side by side with Zeb, and inevitably everyone's eyes were flicking between the two men, judging the proof. Except Dom's eyes weren't; he still concentrated solely on Aidan.

"Stupid arse," he said fondly. "You think I can't tell you from anyone else on the planet? Maybe the pair of you had me confused at first, especially if I didn't get a good look. But whatever the fuck your name is, I know for certain you're the man I went to bed with. And the one I'd want back there if there was any goddamn chance."

There was another, far more shocked silence.

Someone cleared their throat, slowly and deliberately. An elegantly dressed older woman stepped to the front of the crowd that surrounded Dominic and the twins.

"Jesus Christ," Dominic groaned.

"No," she said in a sharp, well-educated voice. "As you should well know. I'm just your mother."

The air crackled with the single snap of a camera flash. Immediately Titus swung around to face the photographer in question and roared, "Out! All of you! Right *now*!"

And, astoundingly, they all filed out.

Chapter Thirty

THE ensuing quiet in the studio was a welcome contrast, with just a select few people remaining. At least Aidan knew them all personally. The press were probably lying in wait outside the front door of the agency—where Titus and Lukas had bustled them out like two of the most professional London club security men Zeb said he'd ever seen—but Aidan felt at last there was enough calm for him to get his thoughts straight. He drew a couple of chairs away from the group and sat down, hoping to catch up on news with Zeb. Someone turned Dominic's slideshow on again and it had the same mesmerizing effect as the first time around. Dominic had seated his mother in one of the armchairs and sat down beside her to talk. Tanya and Eric had joined them. Wendy and Gerald were giggling over something in the back row of the audience chairs.

"Ade?" Zeb eased himself into the chair beside him. He looked surprisingly disturbed. "I'm sorry about all this."

Aidan shook his head. "It's okay. It was always going to happen." He hugged Zeb briefly. "At least you're back. Are things okay with Lukas?"

"He's fine. Meant to be taking it easy, which makes me feel even more guilty about today."

"And you two as a couple?"

"I've worn him down with my dogged pursuit." Zeb couldn't resist a small smirk. "I think he sees me in a different light now. At the very least, we're a work in progress, and the progress is all in the right direction."

"I'm pleased for you."

"Ade." Zeb wriggled on the chair, crossing his slender legs, then uncrossing them again. "You know what you said over there? You more or less declared your love for H-G."

Aidan grimaced. "Don't remind me." Maybe no one had been paying close enough attention, and even if they had…. "People will forget that nonsense soon enough."

"Not sure H-G will," Zeb said. He cleared his throat. "And that's partly why Lukas and I decided to stay for the conference. H-G saw us in the hallway earlier today. Me and Lukas. Kissing. He thought… well, from the look on his face, he thought I was you."

"Oh. *Oh*." Aidan had wondered how this day could get any worse, and now he was finding out.

The door of the studio banged open. "I found the free wine!" Titus called gleefully. He'd ostensibly left to find the toilet, but now returned carrying a crate of assorted wine.

"Damn good idea," Lukas said, and started helping Titus open the first few bottles. "I think we could all do with some moral support at the moment." He opened a cabinet at the back of the studio and took out a box of glasses. He'd barely put a few out on the table before Tanya swooped in and grabbed one.

Smiling, Lukas filled her glass almost to the brim. Claudio was close on her heels, and Tanya dashed back to her seat as if afraid she was coming in for more criticism. Lukas looked at Claudio shrewdly. "I'm Lukas Stefanowicz," he said and offered Claudio his hand. "I arranged the deal with Zeb in the first place, and I'm only sorry I wasn't here to see it through personally."

"It's been a very confusing day," Claudio said. He took a deep drink, and barely noticed Lukas topping it up again.

"I don't think we should let our clients' personal relationships disproportionately influence what's been a very successful campaign," Lukas said smoothly. "Both Zeb and Dom have benefitted from the exposure, and I notice your company's stock has risen several points since Dom's return. I believe you'll be showing many of these astounding photos in your stores?"

"Yes, indeed." Claudio's gaze moved to a spectacular view over the Eiger's north face. "They're going to be an exclusive feature."

"Excellent result. And maybe we can discuss Zeb modeling for you sometime," Lukas added. "At a special fee, of course."

"To be honest," Claudio said slowly, his good humor apparently quite restored, "I've seen a few shots on YouTube of the model I thought was Zeb—and we're quite impressed with *him*. We have another swimwear range coming out soon, named for our British Olympic swimmers. We'd certainly consider him as an option for modeling support on the campaign."

"And we'd certainly love to have him on our books," Lukas said. He looked at Aidan and raised his eyebrows. "A change of career, Aidan?"

Aidan yelped. "No! Oh my God, no. I mean, thank you for the compliment." *Modeling? Me?* He could see the glint in Lukas's eye as if he were already framing shots. "No thanks," he said firmly. "Those days are over for me."

DOM left his mother chatting with the others. Claudio had wandered over to the armchairs, and actually had his arm around Tanya's shoulders at that moment. Dom hoped she was relaxing after all the shock. He caught Eric's eye, and when Eric winked at him, Dom winked back. And then Eric, too, looked as shocked as if he'd been hit by a cricket bat.

Dom slid onto the vacant chair beside Aidan. The other twin—the real Zeb, Dom was going to have to get used to that—was snuggling up close to the older bloke, Lukas, over by the drinks. Maybe the older bloke had some kind of immunity to that bloody sweater.

"I saw them snogging," Dom said to Aidan. "The real Zeb and his man. I thought it was you."

"I know. He told me." Aidan looked relieved yet upset. "How could you have thought I—?"

"Let's not go there," Dom said quickly. "It was just for a stupid, jealous moment. I wasn't thinking or looking properly. I was an arse, and I know it."

"No." Aidan sighed. "I'm as bad. I thought once you got your funding, you wouldn't be bothered about dating me. And what Tanya said seemed to confirm it. Plus I knew how you'd react when you found out I wasn't even Zeb."

"You did, did you?" Dom said cheerfully. "You knew I'd say 'fuck that'?"

"You'd…?" Aidan looked like he didn't know whether to laugh or cry. "Don't try and make me feel better, Dominic. I felt an idiot and a fraud, especially on that first date. But then… I found I didn't want to stop."

They were silent for a moment. Dom shifted on his seat, suddenly restless. "Did you lie about everything?"

"Of course not."

"What about the *going too far*?" He waggled his eyebrows. It was their code for sexual innuendo. The sudden, answering light in Aidan's eyes made hope leap in Dom's chest like a caged tiger seeking release.

"No. Not *that*." Aidan smiled. "Far from it. That was the most real part of everything."

"Thank God for that. Best bloody sex I ever had."

Aidan gave a small gasp. "I…. That's the case for me as well."

Dom reached for Aidan's hand and was absurdly happy when Aidan curled his fingers into Dom's palm. "So what exactly do you do, if you're not a model like your brother?"

"Something simple. I'm a playwright and director. Wendy and Titus are in my theater group."

"That's not simple at all." Dom was impressed. "No wonder you were so touchy about the movies we saw."

"Not touchy." Aidan gave a small but—in Dom's opinion—exciting smile. "Sensitive, remember?"

Dom laughed. "You were a bloody good model, though."

"No, I wasn't."

Dom snorted. "Enough of the false modesty. You acted more confidently as Zeb."

Aidan's smile grew. "You're right. Maybe I should continue to channel that."

"Maybe you should. Enough, at least, for an exclusive modeling assignment. With an audience of one."

Aidan laughed. "You, I assume?"

"Bright boy."

Aidan's hand had tightened in his. Dom really hoped this was a good sign that they had a second chance. But what did he know about this romance crap? Then he caught sight of Gerald peering at him from the other side of the room, with a large glass of wine in his hand. Gerald nodded toward Aidan, winked at Dom, and gave him a thumbs-up.

That was good enough encouragement for Dom.

"I meant what I said," Dom murmured. "I don't care what your bloody name is. I know *you*."

Aidan flushed. "It's been both hard and easy to be Zeb, you know? I haven't enjoyed being in the public eye, but at least I was interesting and glamorous when I was Zeb."

Dom growled. He didn't know exactly where the sound came from, but it was heartfelt. "Why the hell do you do that? Compare yourself? I'm sure your twin is a perfectly good bloke—"

"I can't remember ever hearing Zeb described in those terms."

"—but he's not you."

Aidan was still red. "Of course not, he's much more—"

"Stop right there!" Dom drew a breath. He'd seen Tanya's head lift as if her Dom-dar had kicked into action at his raised voice. "I don't know what the hell you're going to say, but don't. You're an individual. A very special and attractive one. The only one I want, anyway."

Zeb and Lukas were approaching. Dom turned to look at the model. Zeb was tall, graceful, and gorgeous, but Dom wondered how he could ever have mistaken that for Aidan's much more natural, and beautiful, fascination. "Zeb, is your brother always this bad at taking compliments?"

Zeb smiled. "Yes, he is. And without justification."

Lukas looked at Aidan, concerned. "Aidan, I'm sorry. I had no idea Zeb had cooked up this ridiculous scheme. I didn't expect him to come with me to Switzerland, and to be honest, I was angry at first. If I'd known he'd also tricked you into acting as him, I'd have been even more annoyed."

"Not exactly *tricked*—" Zeb started.

"He gave me the fee," Aidan protested at the same time, then flushed even deeper red. "Oh God, how humiliating is that?" He flashed an anguished, sideways look at Dom, then rushed on, "I know you always offer to help me financially, Lukas, and so does Zeb. But I need to make it on my own. All it needs is a few more theater bookings and we'll be self-sufficient, and my teaching income covers most everything else."

Dom listened with rapt interest. It sounded like Aidan was living on the breadline. He felt an unfamiliar feeling ambush him—the need to care for someone, even if he wasn't entirely sure how to carry it out. But Dom would make sure Aidan never ate anything but the best roast beef in the future.

Zeb pulled over another chair and sat. "Another reason I came here was to see if Benjy was around. He's—"

"We know Benjy," Dom interrupted. "And he knows us." He glanced at Aidan and tried not to laugh. If Aidan got any redder, he'd combust.

"Yeah? Great! I wanted to talk to him about an idea Lukas and I had. We have a client who wants to film a promotional video: a play within a play. He's been looking to us for extras, but he actually needs a proper production team, including a playwright and director."

"I know several good ones—" Aidan began.

Dom only just restrained himself from slapping the obtuse kid on the head.

"You," Zeb said with a laugh. "I recommended you. The guy doesn't want Tarantino and, to be honest, can't afford someone like that. He wants someone who appreciates and understands theater, who's talented of course, but who's just waiting for a big break."

"That's you," Dom said with satisfaction.

"You've never even seen any of my work," Aidan retorted, but his eyes were shining. "Zeb, Lukas—the client isn't CCC, is it?"

Zeb laughed loudly. "Heavens, no. Though it'd certainly save money on costumes. No, they're professional costumiers. Really well known in the business, just not in the wider media. It's a breakthrough campaign for them."

"Wow," Aidan said.

Dom could see Aidan wanted to say yes but had this stupid self-deprecation thing going. He wondered if a friendly thump on the arm would help.

"I know you don't want charity," Lukas said. "This wouldn't be, believe me. This is a proper paying gig and may get you noticed by people in the theater. It could be a big breakthrough for you too."

"What about the Dreamweavers?" Aidan asked.

Lukas smiled gently. "There will be background parts for them if appropriate, I'm sure."

"A part in a movie? That sounds marvelous, Shakespeare." Titus appeared suddenly and startlingly behind Lukas. "Who'd you have to sleep with to get that, then?" He chortled, until Wendy stamped on his foot and he yelped. She grabbed his arm, her eyes shining, which may have been either from the wine Titus had been pouring copiously into her glass or the fact that Gerald still had his arm around her waist. "You can tell us about it later. We're all off to the pub now." The rest of the group stood clustered behind her.

"Wait for us," Lukas said.

Zeb sprang to his feet at once. Dom and Aidan stood as well, and Aidan hugged Zeb.

"Thank you for the recommendation. It's marvelous. And thank you, Lukas."

"I'm here for you both, Aidan," Lukas said. "I love you the same as Zeb."

"Not *quite* the same, surely?" Zeb looked piqued.

"Be quiet," Lukas said, not loudly but very firmly. "We will talk about that later, not here."

Dom was amused to see Aidan's twin looking abashed. Then he caught Zeb's gaze over Lukas's shoulder, and Zeb gave him an exaggerated wink and a gesture that implied he was wriggling in a set of handcuffs. *Good God.* Dom didn't envy Lukas the job of managing that twin.

"Dominic?" It was his mother's coolest tone. "Please introduce us properly."

Dom swallowed carefully. God only knew how the old dear could always make him feel ten years old. "This is Ze—Aidan."

"Pleased to meet you, Mrs. Hartington-George," Aidan said.

Dom didn't see how his mother could resist those wide-open eyes, though maybe it was a gay thing. Aidan glanced at him with nervous trust, as if checking he was doing the right thing, and Dom's cock thickened. *Dammit... it's obviously a* sex *thing, and should never be mentioned to my mother at all.* He surreptitiously adjusted his crotch while his mother shook Aidan's hand, at her most polite.

"It's not unusual for you to confuse the names of the young men who accompany you, Dominic," she said. Her tone was much warmer in the light of Aidan's smile. "But it is unusual for you to introduce them to me."

"Aidan is a very unusual man, Mother. I want you both to get along. Please."

She was obviously startled at the passion in his voice. "Good Lord," she said quietly to Aidan. "It appears you really *are* unusual."

Dom slid his arm around Aidan's waist. "Look. I don't do the hearts-and-flowers thing. Never wanted it myself, never needed it."

"I can imagine." Aidan raised his eyebrows.

"But you bring me the zest I only ever got from climbing. Makes me want to say things I never have before."

"Oh good grief," Eric groaned.

Dom reached out and clapped his hand over Eric's mouth. "Go to the pub, punk, and take everyone else with you. I want to be alone with Aidan."

"You paying?" Eric asked unabashed, though he skipped out of Dom's reach as he said it.

"No. I am," Claudio said with a grin of his own.

Zeb grasped Aidan's hands. "You're still an item? You and Dom? Please tell me yes."

"Yes," Aidan said softly.

"By God, yes!" Dom said much more robustly.

Wendy gave a whoop and slapped hands with Titus. "Told you it'd be all right on the night! That's *another* tenner you owe me," she crowed.

"So which pub are we going to?" Dom's mother said in her clipped tones. "I'm rather fond of the fruit beers at the Princess Louise."

DOM and Aidan were left alone in the studio. Dom wondered if the blue briefs were still in a drawer there somewhere, but he didn't want to break the mood by rummaging around for them. He'd buy Aidan a bagful of them, come Christmas.

"You were always the more honest one," Aidan said. "Thank you for forgiving my subterfuge."

"Nothing to forgive. You just forgot to be yourself for a while. Everything's straightened out now."

"I let you down."

Dom wanted to kiss him, and maybe also to shut him up, but something told him Aidan needed to get this off his chest. "You never let me down. You've been the making of me."

"And the stupid deal—?"

"Fuck the deal!" Dom cried. "I find the truth always works best for me. Much less danger of fucking things up." He caught the worried look on Aidan's face and his heart missed a beat. "I'm being stupid. Facile.

Thoughtless. Tell me whatever I'm doing wrong and I'll stop doing it."

Aidan smiled, but a little sadly. "What I said earlier, when I was trying to get everyone to shut up. I didn't know I'd... you know? I wasn't thinking. I'm sorry if I embarrassed you." He peered at Dom's expression, obviously struggling with his own embarrassment.

"I love you," Dom said.

Aidan winced. "Well, I didn't say those words exactly."

"No." Dom realized the young man needed to acclimatize himself better to Dom's unique style of brutal honesty. "I mean, that's what *I* say."

"You?" Aidan seemed stricken, though his eyes were attractively bright.

"I may have said it before, when I was shagged out," Dom went on, rather pleased to see the flush rise again on Aidan's cheeks. "Maybe a few times when you were asleep. And Gerald may have dragged it out of me when we were pissed together. I just needed to say it to your face."

"But you heard me admit I did it for the money. At first, anyway."

Dom shrugged. "So did I. But if I had to make the choice between the bloody money and you, I'd give it all back right now." He drew Aidan tightly against him. He felt Aidan's wiry chest relax against his torso, his slender thigh pushing between Dom's wider ones, and his hands sliding down Dom's back to cup his arse. Dom kissed him. The delight of tasting Aidan's mouth after weeks away was a tantalizing promise. Delight, desire, demand. Everything he remembered from before his trip and everything he longed for in the future. Aidan slid his tongue into Dom's mouth, teasing and reaching, and his soft gasps crept into Dom as if he wanted to possess him, for them to become one.

Dom broke the kiss because of an inconvenient need to breathe. They stared at each other, chuckling and breathing heavily. "Do you want to follow them to the pub?" Dom asked Aidan.

"No. Let's go straight to your place. And... I know where Sven put the blue briefs. If you want me to fetch them, that is. Take them home with us."

Home. How good that sounds. Dom stared happily down into Aidan's shining, smiling face. "That thing about giving back the money if I had to choose?"

"Yes?" Aidan whispered, perhaps a little worriedly.

"You'd be worth every damn penny," Dom said.

Now Available

www.dreamspinnerpress.com

Coming in December 2016

#23

Catching Heir by Julia Talbot

Is he in love with an old hotel—or its new owner?

Professional snowboarder Cullen Patrick is successful and kinda famous. So when he inherits an old Colorado hotel from an unknown relative, he really should leave well enough alone.

Matt Nathanson has been managing the Treeline Estates since college. He loved the elderly former owner, and he stands to inherit the place if no one claims it in the next week. Of course, Cullen shows up, and Matt thinks it's time to move on. He doesn't want to like Cullen, no matter how engaging the guy is, or how hunky.

Cullen has grand ideas for the Treeline, but he doesn't want to implement them without Matt, and he's not sure he's ready to give up snowboarding. Can Matt convince Cullen that putting down roots is worth it… and maybe catch his heir at the same time?

#24

Striking Sparks by Ari McKay

The stakes are high and the heat is on.

Beau Walker, owner of the Barbecue Shack, needs the help of Jake Parnell, his one-time rival and secret crush, in a televised barbecue competition. Beau is a proud man, but the stakes are high, and smart, sexy Jake is his only hope, even if being around Jake reawakens the attraction he's fought for years.

Jake left his hometown, determined to build a life somewhere his sexuality wouldn't hurt his family's restaurant business—and far away from hunky, obstinate Beau Walker. Then after his twin, Josh, is killed, Jake returns to support his brother's wife and children. Despite his reservations, he agrees to go head-to-head against Beau on national television. Between stress and grief, as well as pride and determination, only one thing is certain—the heat between Beau and Jake extends well beyond the kitchen.

www.dreamspinnerpress.com

Lightning Source UK Ltd.
Milton Keynes UK
UKHW040604281119
354396UK00001B/2/P